THE INTERSTELLAR DETECTIVES 3

P.J. Nichols

The Interstellar Detectives 3
Copyright © 2025 by P.J. Nichols

Published by Brilliant Owl Press
All rights reserved.

No part of this book may be reproduced in any form or by any electronic or mechanical means including information storage and retrieval systems, without permission in writing from the author, except for the use of brief quotations in a book review.

This book is a work of fiction. Names, characters, places, and incidents either are products of the author's imagination or are used fictitiously. Any resemblance to actual persons, living or dead, events, or locales is entirely coincidental.

Paperback ISBN 978-4-910091-68-6

pjnichols.com

Cover design by Thomas Paehler

*To readers who love puzzling mysteries
and nail-biting quests,
I hope you enjoy the latest part of Screed's adventure!*

CHAPTER 1

Although Screed had told himself to do his packing well in advance and in an organized fashion (to allow the last few days of his summer break to be laid back), he procrastinated until 11:00 p.m. the night before his departure.

Since there was no time to *carefully fold* all his clothes, he was haphazardly stuffing item after item into his big bag (and shaking his head at himself for, once again, putting off packing until the last minute...)

Screed's growth spurt was now in full swing, so a significant portion of the clothes he was jamming into his overstuffed bag had been newly purchased over the past week. (And his mom had intentionally bought slightly oversized clothing, to ensure he wouldn't outgrow anything while in Year 3 at The Academy.)

Screed was neither excited about nor dreading his upcoming ten months at the special school he'd attended for two years already. He knew hanging out with Vlad would be cool—as it had always been since they met as toddlers. Plus, Florence was incredibly imaginative and original when it came to advice and suggestions for new music compositions, so Screed was looking forward to spending a decent amount of time in the music room after classes and on weekends.

Even though those things would be fun, there was something he was *unexpectedly* looking forward to... He had heard through the rumor mill that Zora "might kind of like him," and for a reason he didn't fully comprehend yet, the thought of starting a boyfriend-girlfriend relationship with her had been on his mind all summer long. (He only hoped that she hadn't had a change of heart during the 2-month summer break... as that would mean any chance of dating her would be over before it could even start!)

* * *

During the first part of their journey to The Academy (an 8-hour flight), Screed needed some advice from Vlad about what he should or shouldn't do when first seeing Zora.

"Are you 110% sure she likes me?" Screed asked his best friend again.

"Dude, she totally digs you," Vlad replied. "I talked to Flo a few times a week for the whole summer: Flo and Zora called each other almost every day, and Zora apparently asked about you during EVERY SINGLE call."

"How do I approach her when we arrive tomorrow?" Screed asked. "I mean, I can't just walk up and ask her if she wants to go out with me."

Vlad started laughing. "Dude, I am certainly not on expert on relationships," he commented. "I always figured *I'd* be asking *you* for help."

"Well, you and Flo are a couple, right?" Screed said back. "That definitely makes you at least semi-qualified to advise me."

"If you're going to keep pestering me for advice," Vlad—who was not bothered in the least—said, smiling. "Then I guess all I can say is, umm... be yourself, show interest, but don't try to act cool or go overboard."

"Go overboard?" Screed inquired, wanting clarification.

"Like don't suddenly give her a dozen roses out of nowhere," Vlad answered. "That'd probably scare her off."

* * *

After four and a half hours of flying—meaning they were well past the halfway point—the two boys woke up from their naps at more or less the same time.

"Dude, you drooled on yourself while sleeping," Vlad laughed, pointing at the wet patch on Screed's shirt.

"Oops," Screed said after looking down. "No big deal; My shirt's navy, it won't be noticeable once it's dry."

Before Screed had a chance to ask more questions about *"the wild world of dating,"* Vlad started up a discussion about a completely different topic.

"Think we've got any chance at being picked for the Elite 7?" Vlad asked Screed.

"Us?" Screed reacted, surprised. "I thought everyone selected was usually in Year 5 or 6."

"They often are," Vlad—who had obviously studied up on this thoroughly—replied. "But a few Year 3s and 4s have been chosen in the past."

* * *

The Elite 7 was a special program—which involved every teacher nominating the students they felt were "motivated, skilled problem-solvers, who seemed destined to do great things after graduating."

Basically, a week before the summer break was set to finish, all teachers from the previous academic year came to The Academy for a big meeting: and one part of that included each teacher submitting the names of the two students they were nominating for the upcoming year's Elite 7 program.

There were no restrictions on rank or year, so it was technically possible for all selected to be Rank 3, or for everyone to be in the same year.

The "winners" were simply the seven students who had received the most nominations. (And in the case of a tie for the seventh spot, the headmaster had the authority to pick who would go—or permit an eighth participant if she thought both deserved it.)

* * *

"Dude, the Elite 7 has gotta be the coolest opportunity The Academy offers," Vlad explained excitedly. "They get to go to a far-off planet, for close to a month, to do practical training and tests which are based on actual missions that happened in the past."

"Well, technically we've already been on two real missions," Screed pointed out. "Wouldn't the teachers want to pick students who could benefit from it more than us?"

"Possibly," Vlad admitted. "But I hope you're wrong. I would love to get a month of practical training. Plus, almost everyone who has been in the Elite 7 program has gone on to a great career."

"Well, we'll know pretty soon," Screed smiled. "They announce the Elite 7 list during the big welcome ceremony. ... But if I were you, I wouldn't get my hopes up."

"I'll try not to," Vlad sighed.

CHAPTER 2

This year's big welcome ceremony and dinner was no different than the ones they'd attended in their first two years.

Screed, Vlad, and Florence were sitting together at the long table for all Year 3s, and they elected to sit relatively close to the front—to get a better view of the teachers at the head table. (There were no assigned seats for students—only assigned tables—so Screed and his friends had shown up early to get their pick of location.)

* * *

"Next," Headmaster Vela announced loudly from the front podium after the dinner was wrapped up. "We'll be unveiling the selections for this year's Elite 7. Those whose names are called, please come join me up front."

"The moment we've been waiting for," Vlad—who had his fingers crossed—whispered to Screed and Florence.

"Following with tradition," the headmaster went on, "I'll say the names in order of year, starting with Year 6s. So, without further ado, let's begin. ... Year 6... Charlotte!"

The table of Year 6 boys and girls erupted in applause as Charlotte embarrassingly went up to stand next to the headmaster.

"You guys know what her power is, right?" Vlad asked Screed and Florence.

"Of course," Florence replied. "She can make her body become as thin as a sheet of paper."

"I've heard about that, too," Screed said. "And she can then even roll herself up like a scroll, or fold herself over and over and end up being a pocketbook."

"For Year 5," Headmaster Vela went on. "Dax!"

"He's a very unique Rank 3," Vlad explained to his friends. "One of his hands has super speed, and the other has super strength."

"Neat," Screed nodded.

"Now onto Year 4," the headmaster continued. "Zora!"

"Woohoo!" Screed cheered, hoping she would notice this as she approached the front.

"Guys," Vlad then said softly to his friends. "That's only three so far; That means the final four are Year 3s."

Vlad wasn't the only person who was surprised at this development; Over half of the students could be heard murmuring about why this might be happening.

"And now, Year 3," the headmaster said, rechecking the list in her left hand. "Florence, Screed, and Vlad!"

The entire Year 3 table roared with excitement, loving the fact that three from their grade had been picked for this honor.

Vlad pumped his fists; This was awesome. More than awesome.

"But that's only six in total," Florence said as they stood up to walk to the stage. "That means a Year 2 has been chosen."

"And finally," Headmaster Vela continued with a big grin on her face. "For the first time in the Elite 7's long and respected history, a Year 2 has been earned a spot. Come on up... Vivian!"

The expression on Vivian's face was a cross between elation and disbelief. She was so surprised that she briefly remained seated, and the kids sitting beside her had to remind her she was supposed to go up to the front.

Screed looked over at Rudd Major—who was at the far end of the teacher's table—and could see the tears welling up in his eyes. His granddaughter was making him prouder and prouder by the day.

"A round of applause for our Elite 7!" the headmaster said loudly (while initiating the clapping.) "Congratulations!"

* * *

Headmaster Vela had instructed the seven selected pupils to stick around in the big hall after everyone else had left (following dessert and the closing announcements.)

"Once again," she said to the excited group of seven teens. "Congratulations on being selected."

"You all earned these selections thanks to your effort and dedication to excellence," Mr. Fenelon—the vice principal—added. "And we look forward to hearing how your upcoming month of practical training go."

"You will be departing at the start of next week," Headmaster Vela outlined. "Meaning you'll be able to attend the first week of classes here before you go."

"And just in case you were about to ask," Mr. Fenelon said next. "You will be expected to keep up on regular class work during your month there. Your teachers will give you lists of which pages to study and which assignments to complete."

"Headmaster Vela," Screed asked. "I was just wondering, umm… if there are any new Rank 1s at the Academy? Year 1s will be at orientation all week, so if any of them happen to be Rank 1s, I wouldn't have a chance to meet them. You know, because I'll be gone when they start joining classes from next week."

"The answer to your question is a happy one, Mr. Palin," the headmaster replied. "We have two new Rank 1s, identical twin sisters."

"Cool," Zora (also a Rank 1) smiled.

"But their ability has a twist we've never seen before," Headmaster Vela went on, "which seems to be related to the fact that they are twins: Their mind reading powers only work when they are together; When separated by more than a few meters, their powers fade to nothing."

"And while that might sound negative or discouraging," Mr. Fenelon added. "There is a bright side; Their mind reading strength functions at double that of a typical Rank 1."

"So, individually they have no power," Screed said, wanting to confirm he understood clearly. "But when together, double power?"

"We were as intrigued as you when we first learned about it," Mr. Fenelon admitted. "And I have a feeling the twins are destined for great things."

CHAPTER 3

As they had agreed before heading to their separate dorms yesterday evening, Screed and Zora met up in the hallway twenty minutes before the breakfast buffet would start today.

They then began making their way to the entrance of the dorm the twins were staying in. (Their plan was to stand just outside the entrance, and wait for the twins to walk out—and then invite them to eat breakfast together.)

"One's called Emily and the other's called Trina," Zora reminded Screed. "And remember, we just want to welcome them and see if they want to hang out for a bit: don't start bombarding them with questions about their powers."

"Yes, boss," Screed smiled, saluting Zora in jest. "I'll let you do most of the talking."

* * *

"Talk about *identical,*" Screed said softly to Zora when he saw the twins—who had the exact same facial features, height, and hair—emerge from the dorm.

"Emily and Trina, right?" Zora said while approaching them with a big smile. "I'm Zora, and this is Screed. We're also Rank 1s, and just came by to welcome you to The Academy."

"We certainly know who you two are," one of the twins said back. "We saw both of you get selected for the Elite 7 yesterday."

"I was pretty shocked when *my name* was called," Zora admitted. "But Screed here is a superstar, though."

(That comment got both girls giggling a bit: which was a nice way to break the ice.)

Since the daily breakfast buffet was a *come-and-go-as-you-please* set-up, students weren't required to sit at the assigned tables they used at lunches and dinners.

The doors had only been open for a few minutes when they walked in, so they could choose any place in the entire hall.

"Let's sit over there," Zora said, leading the way. "That's the only spot where the morning sunshine comes in."

"And we all need our daily dose of vitamin D," Screed commented. "Helps keep our immune systems strong."

(But Screed immediately realized he was the only one laughing at that "clever" comment!)

"Screed isn't known for his jokes, as you can tell," Zora then said as a way to bail Screed out.

...

Although their appearance was identical, their personalities couldn't have been more different. Trina was the bold, straight-talking, loud type. And Emily was shy and soft-spoken, and didn't say much other than just nodding to agree with her sister's opinion.

"Our characters aren't our only difference," Trina pointed out when she had finished about half of her food. "Our academic skills are hugely different: Me being the poor performer, and Emily being the genius."

"Our friend Vlad is a genius, too," Zora told Emily. "We're so glad he'll finally have someone who can follow along with what he's talking about."

Emily smiled upon hearing that. And then she made her first comment of the morning. "What subjects is he good at?" she asked.

"Pretty much everything," Screed replied. "But he especially loves anything related to *'Rules and Regulations of The Interstellar Detective Agency.'*"

"Well, maybe Emily can give him a run for his money," Trina joked. "She has had her head buried in Academy textbooks from the day we learned of our powers."

* * *

The breakfast hour was now about half over, so the hall was getting fuller and fuller. Screed's group had finished eating and were now on their second cup of tea.

"I haven't reached the chapter on the Elite 7 yet," Emily (a lot less timid now) said. "What exactly happens in that program?"

"Well, Vlad can answer that question a lot better than me or Zora," Screen said. "But he filled me in on the basics: The Elite 7 members spend a month on a planet called Zerasta, which is approximately a 12-hour flight from Vos."

"A whole month?" Emily inquired. "And will you do special lessons or something like that?"

"From what Vlad explained," Screed went on. "The seven members are randomly split up into two teams every day: one of 3 and one of 4. Then each team is given an identical case, or challenge or puzzle, to solve."

"Oh, so it's a race to see who solves it first?" Emily asked.

"Kind of yes and kind of no," Screed replied. "The goal isn't just to solve each one as quickly as possible: the focus is to tackle each challenge in the safest and most logical way possible, while considering the various abilities each team member has."

"And since they switch up the groups every day," Zora added, "you have to rethink your approach each time."

"Sounds cool," Emily smiled. "I hope Trina and I get picked for that sometime before we graduate."

"When do you guys depart?" Trina then asked.

"Six days from today," Zora answered. "But our teachers will be assigning us a month's worth of homework to take with us."

Since they'd been here for quite some time now, they decided to get up and head back to their dorms (to prep for the start of the school day.)

"It was really nice meeting you two," Zora said while picking up the four empty teacups. "We'll see you in Rank 1 class in about five weeks."

"We can't wait to hear about the Elite 7 stuff you get to do," Emily said while getting ready to leave the table.

"Hey," Trina then said as they all started walking out. "I know this is none of my business, but are you two a couple? Or just good friends?"

Screed immediately felt uncomfortable... (But thankfully, Zora answered first!)

"I'd say we're *friends on our way to becoming a couple,*" she told the twins. "Screed, wouldn't you agree?"

(Hurry up and say something, Screed!)

"Yeah, I'd say that sounds about right," he said awkwardly.

"Glad to hear it," Trina smiled. "You guys would make a nice couple."

CHAPTER 4

Rudd Major happily volunteered to fly this year's Elite 7 to Zerasta. (And he would also stay the entire month, just in case one of the kids had a health issue and needed to be quickly brought back to Vos.)

A few hours into their long flight, Charlotte—who was clearly the most social of the seven kids—decided it'd be fun to do some games to allow everyone a chance to get more comfortable with each other.

...

After a few fun, ice breaker games, Charlotte then suggested they each share a story.

"Alright," she said to everyone. "We will each tell about our most embarrassing experience to date at The Academy. ... Everyone up for that?"

No one protested, although not everyone was sure they had a story that could be classified as *embarrassing*.

"And to take the pressure off," she went on, "I'll go first." She then spun around to Rudd Major and said, "You may want to put earplugs in, so your image of us being ideal students doesn't get tarnished."

Rudd Major started laughing. "I have an even better idea," he said while standing up. "We're flying on autopilot, so I'll go to my quarters for a nap. ... But if anything starts flashing on the pilot's panel, come and wake me immediately."

...

"This story," Charlotte began, "happened back when I was in Year 4. You all, of course, know Kase—and most of you are aware of how much he used to tease and terrorize other students. Well, one day, a few friends and I came up with a good idea of how to get some revenge on him..."

"I like the sound of this," Zora—who had been putting up with Kase's rude antics and insensitive behavior in Rank 1 class for years—smiled.

"The plan was relatively simple," Charlotte explained. "Right after the last class one day, I bolted to the hallway, used my power to make my body paper thin, and folded myself a bunch of times until I was about 10 by 20 centimeters—meaning I basically looked like a notebook. A friend of mine then picked me up off the floor, went back into the class as everyone was packing their stuff up, and slipped me into Kase's bag. We figured he'd be heading back to his dorm, where he'd probably drop his bag in the dorm's common room before going to get a snack or something to drink."

"Let me guess," Zora grinned. "You were going to revert to normal, and scare the living daylights out of him when he came back to sit down."

"Exactly," she nodded. "But Stef, the girl who had placed me in Kase's bag, made a grave error... She had accidentally put me in his gym bag instead of his school bag. Kase carried both bags back to his dorm, dropped his school bag in the common room there, and then took his gym bag straight to the boys' changing room beside the exercise ground."

"Oh my..." Vivian commented. "So, what did you do?"

"Well," she went on. "I could hear the other boys changing into their gym clothes, but when taking his shorts and t-shirt out of his bag, Kase didn't notice *me* in there. ... And before I knew it, he put his bag in a locker and locked it!"

"Woah," Vlad commented. "But you can't switch back to normal while in a locker, right?"

"Correct," she replied. "I had to just wait there, in paper form, while he trained outside for the next ninety minutes."

"That's awful," Florence commented.

"But what happened next was 100 times worse than that," Charlotte went on. "When Kase and the offers finally came back an hour and a half later, he unlocked his locker, took his bag out and put it on a bench, and then reached in to take out a towel to go shower. But since I was right beside the towel, he pulled me out too, without noticing. Then—just like any notebook would—I fell to the floor. And since my face was folded into the middle, I couldn't see what was going on."

"You were on the dirty floor of the boys' changing room?" Vivian reacted. "Someone surely must have spotted you there, though?"

"Well," she told her keen audience. "Since I could hear what was happening, I was aware when everyone returned from the shower. One of the boys noticed *me* on the floor, and since I looked like a notebook, he asked the others if anyone had dropped something. ... And when no one claimed *me* as theirs, one boy suggested to '*put it over by the sinks, so the rightful owner would spot it before leaving.*' ... He did exactly that: he put me on the counter near the sinks. But..."

"But?" Zora asked, intrigued.

"But there was some water where he had placed me," she continued. "And, at that time, I didn't know that getting wet caused me to immediately revert to normal."

"Oh no!" Vivian exclaimed.

"All of a sudden, I was back to being a person, sitting on the counter next to the sinks!" she groaned. "Thank goodness all the boys were wearing towels, though."

"But the sinks are pretty close to the entrance," Dax pointed out. "They probably assumed you had just run into the changing room."

"That's exactly what they thought," Charlotte explained, face beet red just from remembering the experience. "And I was so shocked and confused that I didn't even try explaining what had really happened. I just bolted out, and then avoided any eye-contact with those boys for weeks."

"Did you ever tell them the truth?" Screed asked.

"A month or so after it happened, I tried telling Kase," Charlotte replied. "But he didn't believe me."

"That story takes the gold medal when it comes to embarrassment," Zora told Charlotte. "I couldn't have continued attending The Academy if that happened to me."

CHAPTER 5

"Welcome to Zerasta!" Ms. Morg—one of the two instructors in charge of running the Elite 7 program—said loudly as the kids began walking off Rudd Major's ship. "You all come with me, and Mr. Derringer will assist Rudd Major with unloading the food."

...

"Wow, this facility is a lot bigger than I expected," Vlad commented in awe while entering the complex. "Looks like this place is made for a hundred students, not seven."

"Some major upgrades were done ten years ago," Ms. Morg explained. "Plus, a new wing was just recently added: And the addition of that wing means you'll have a lot of never-done-before tests and challenges."

She told the kids to leave their bags in the hallway, and guided them into a large meeting room: which had a single, long table in it (similar to what might be in a company boardroom.)

"Sit at the seat where your name card is," she instructed them. "You each have an *Elite 7 Manual* there, plus a diary notebook to record the things you do."

...

"Ms. Morg," Vlad—who was probably going to have more questions than everyone else combined—asked. "I was just wondering: If it's only you and Mr. Derringer here, who prepares all the meals?"

"You haven't even been here for 20 minutes," she laughed, "and you're already thinking about food? Well, the answer to that is very simple: Each day, three of you will be in charge of meal prep and cleanup. The foods you will prepare for breakfast, lunch, and dinner—and detailed instructions about how to cook everything—will be displayed on a monitor in the big kitchen."

...

"Oh, and since were on this topic," she continued after everyone nodded in understanding. "I randomly drew names for our trio of cooks tomorrow: Vlad, Screed, and Dax."

"I hope you guys have a bit of experience in the kitchen," Dax said to Screed and Vlad. "The most complicated thing I've ever cooked is pancakes."

Everyone started laughing.

"I'm not sure pancakes can be referred to as *cooking*," Charlotte joked. "But hey, I have confidence in you guys."

"That's exactly the kind of attitude we want to hear," Ms. Morg commented. "Be supportive of your teammates, and the sky's the limit."

* * *

Roughly half an hour later, Ms. Morg had finished explaining everything on her list: most of which was related to the different parts of the facility, plus safety and emergency procedures.

Rudd Major and Mr. Derringer—having hauled all the rations from the ship to the walk-in freezer and fridge—then joined everyone in the meeting room.

"Impeccable timing," Ms. Morg commented as they came in. "I've just completed the orientation. ... Alright, I want the boys to follow Mr. Derringer. He'll show you to your dorm room. Girls, you come with me."

"Oh, and one final thing," Mr. Derringer added, "which Ms. Morg may have mentioned already: Please think of your entire stay here as a month-long mission; meaning you should follow mission protocol from now until you leave." Then he stopped and turned to face Vivian. "Is mission protocol covered in Year 1?"

"Yes, sir," she replied. "Year 1s learn the protocols during their final two weeks before summer break."

As Screed, Vlad, and Dax began following Mr. Derringer out of the meeting room, Rudd Major joined them too.

Ms. Morg started laughing. "You don't think we'd make you share a room with those three, do you?" she asked him. "We have six individual rooms for teachers and guests, four of which are vacant as it's only me and Mr. Derringer here right now."

"Wonderful," Rudd Major smiled, looking at the map Mr. Derringer had given him a few minutes earlier. "Then I think I'll take myself on a little self-guided tour before turning in for the night. ... What time is breakfast?"

"7:00 a.m. sharp," Mr. Derringer replied. "And just so you know, the three boys will be preparing it."

Rudd Major turned to face Ms. Morg. "I completely agree with having the kids help cook and clean," he told her. "Interstellar Detectives need to be capable not only of solving mysteries, but also of taking care of themselves."

"We certainly think alike," Ms. Morg smiled back.

CHAPTER 6

Screed, Vlad, and Dax—now lying in their respective beds (with the lights off)—were too excited to fall asleep right away.

Dax was an awesome storyteller, and he spent the next thirty minutes telling tales about some of the Year 3 and 4 instructors at The Academy. (They'd only had a week of classes before coming to Zerasta, and therefore knew little other than the curriculum and homework schedule.)

"Sounds like our classes are gonna be way more fun than Year 1 and 2 were," Vlad remarked.

"I think the school intentionally assigns the Year 1 and 2 classes to boring, *by-the-book* type teachers," Dax said back. "To try to keep the focus on academics. ... But yeah, Year 3 is way more entertaining."

"Screed, that sounds cool, eh?" Vlad asked his best friend.

...

"Screed has this skill of going from *active* to *fast asleep* in an instant," Vlad then told Dax.

"Well, maybe we should do the same," Dax said back. "We gotta be up bright and early to prep everyone's breakfast."

* * *

Driiiiing!!

"What the— ?" Screed said in a panic. (He knew he'd been asleep for at least a couple of hours, but it certainly wasn't time to wake up yet.)

"That's not our wake-up call," Vlad told Screed and Dax. "It's the fire alarm."

Dax had had his head under his pillow—as a way to make the noisy alarm a little less painful on his eardrums—but he quickly sat up after hearing Vlad's comment.

Mr. Derringer then opened their dorm door, and (in a panic) said, "Follow me, I'll take us to safety. Once we're there, I'll use my handheld computer to learn where the fire is. C'mon, quickly."

Mr. Derringer was walking as fast as he could, and Screed, Vlad, and Dax did their best to keep up. He led them through a series of corridors, and then down a long set of steps.

"What about the girls?" Screed asked his teacher. "And Rudd Major?"

"Ms. Morg went to get the girls," he replied. "And Rudd Major has a separate evacuation route, which was shown to him shortly after you all arrived."

...

Not long later, they were in a tunnel (that was obviously underground.) ... And the 50-meter-long tunnel led to a door, which, once opened, allowed them to exit the underground. The outdoor area they were now standing in was on a fairly steep slope, presumably on the side of a mountain.

Ms. Morg and the girls were using the same route to evacuate, and they ended up exiting about two minutes after the boys.

"What can you tell us about the fire?" Vlad asked the two instructors. "Are you sure it wasn't a false alarm? I can't see flames anywhere."

Since it was pitch-black outside, Vlad took off his backpack and removed his flashlight.

"Well, at least one person remembered to follow mission

protocol," Rudd Major then commented.

(Rudd Major? When did he get out here??)

Rudd Major, Ms. Morg, and Mr. Derringer then turned on their flashlights and aimed them at the kids.

"Is Vlad the only one of you who brought their backpack when evacuating?" Ms. Morg asked the group.

The kids looked back and forth at each other... Their teacher was correct: only Vlad had a backpack.

Mr. Derringer then aimed a flashlight at his own face, so the kids could see his expressions during the upcoming spiel.

"First of all," he told them. "There is no fire. ... This is a test we do on the first night for every new Elite 7 group. Some of you might think it is cruel and unnecessary. ... However, you all recall how I specifically told you to *treat your time here as a 4-week mission, and follow mission protocol to a T?*"

"And protocol states," Vlad then said, "that an Interstellar Detective should carry his or her supply bag whenever an emergency evacuation occurs."

"I'm sorry," Vivian then said, worried that this mistake might mean she was going to be sent home early.

"No need to fret," Ms. Morg then grinned. "In fact, it has been years since anyone brought a backpack during this little test."

"Eight years, if I recall correctly," Mr. Derringer added. "To be honest, we are ecstatic to see someone succeed this year."

"Alright, now we'll lead you back to your dorms," Ms. Morg said while reentering the tunnel. "And let you all get back to sleep."

"Should we expect more surprises like this?" Vlad inquired while heading into the tunnel.

"Expect the unexpected..." Mr. Derringer laughed. "But don't worry, we'll try not to do any more in the middle of the night. We know how unhealthy it is to sleep less than seven hours."

"I always like to get at least eight," Dax then commented.

Vlad then did some quick math.

"Well, considering you got two hours of sleep already," he told Dax. "If you fall asleep again within fifteen minutes of getting back to our dorm… and sleep right until we wake up to go make breakfast, your total for the night will be about eight."

"You're like a walking and talking computer," Dax commented, laughing. "Sure there's no motherboard in that brain of yours?"

Screed started laughing, too.

"I've asked him the same thing a million times," Screed said. "But alas, Vlad appears to have no computer chips in his head. He's 100% *'person,'* believe it or not."

CHAPTER 7

By the end of their third full day of training, all seven had become fairly accustomed to the daily routine.

Mornings were in-class sessions, and primarily consisted of doing a few "relatively short" tasks; The school had two classrooms, so the two teams were sent to separate rooms to come up with their solutions. (And once the *time to solve* had expired, they'd gather in one room to compare what ideas they'd come up with.)

Afternoons were a lot more fun, because they did more practical, hands-on challenges; Their teachers would set up tasks (some outside, some in the new training wing, some underground), and the two teams—separately, of course—had to complete tasks within restricted time frames. (And since the two teams were randomly decided on at the start of each new school day, everyone had to adapt quickly to cooperating with whoever ended up in their group.)

* * *

The morning session of day 4 was intentionally cut short—thus allowing for an early lunch, since the afternoon task was going to be longer than usual. (And they'd also been told it was *"at least twice as hard"* as what they'd done the previous three days.)

"Team of 4," Ms. Morg said once everyone had finished lunch. "Follow me, please. Team of 3, you're with Mr. Derringer."

Today's team of 4 consisted of Zora, Vlad, Dax, and Charlotte.

The four kids put their small backpacks on and went along with their teacher.

"Where are we headed?" Vlad asked eagerly. "To the new wing again?"

"You're going to be given your task on the front porch of our facility," Ms. Morg replied (assuming this would lead to another question...)

"Oh," Vlad said back, a bit confused. "Then, um—"

"You'll find out more very soon," she smiled back, leading them down the final corridor toward the entrance.

...

Once they were outside, Ms. Morg turned around to give them their instructions.

"Your mission today," she began, "is to rescue an Interstellar Detective team that has been kidnapped. Screed, Vivian, and Florence—of course—will play the role of that team. They are being held at an undisclosed location, which is rigged with a bomb—fictitious, obviously—that will explode in precisely two hours."

She then passed Dax a small, black briefcase, which was a lot heavier than it looked.

"That briefcase," she went on, "is filled with fake diamonds—cubic zirconia to be exact—and you'll understand why when I hand you the ransom note. Oh, and Rudd Major will be playing the role of the *bad guy* today: he's been briefed on what to do. ... Okay, good luck."

After receiving the ransom note from Ms. Morg, Vlad unfolded it and read it to his team.

> *If you want to see these three detectives alive again, deliver 3 kilograms of jewelry-grade diamonds to the shed at coordinates 28.652811°N, 33.192743°E. Once the person at the shed confirms the diamonds'*

authenticity, you'll be provided with the location of your friends. Any tomfoolery, and your friends will be exterminated. The bomb at your friends' holding facility will go off in precisely two hours. It can't be disarmed... so you had better get a move on!

"This mission happened 68 years ago," Ms. Morg said before walking away. "Just like in that mission, you were able to prepare the appropriate weight in *fake* diamonds; Real diamonds, as you can imagine, were not an option."

...

One tool in every Interstellar Detective's kit was a GPS device—which allowed detectives a way to see the longitude and latitude of where they were currently and where they were required to go.

"The shed is about two and a half kilometers up the mountain," Charlotte told the team. "Luckily, vegetation is pretty sparse, so we should be able to take a direct route there."

"Let's jog, but not run," Zora suggested. "And we should stick together the whole time, just in case."

"I agree," Vlad said back. "I'm definitely the least athletic. I'll lead; You guys shouldn't have any trouble keeping up with me."

* * *

Mr. Derringer had instructed Screed, Vivian, and Florence to blindfold themselves, and he was now driving them somewhere.

"You have been kidnapped," Mr. Derringer told them. "The cabin I'll be locking you in has been set up with a fictitious explosive device that will detonate if any of the following three things occur: One, if the door handle is touched. Two, if the camera mounted inside the main room—which will be watching you the entire time—picks up less than 3 bodies for more than 2 minutes. ... (That two minutes is so you to use the washroom when necessary.) And three, if the state-of-the-art mind-reading detector set up there notices a mind reader trying to use his or her powers. ... And by the way, this fictitious bomb will go off in two hours even if not detonated by one of those three things."

CHAPTER 8

"Alright, guys," Dax (who was taking up the rear) said to Vlad, Charlotte, and Zora. "We're getting pretty close. We take a left past that bolder, and then we've only a couple hundred meters to go."

...

After they rounded the bend, they saw the small shack at the end of a path.

"Let's stop here for a sec," Vlad suggested. "We need to come up with a game plan."

"If I go close enough to the cabin," Zora said. "I might be able to read Rudd Major's mind to find out where those three are being held."

"Worth a shot," Vlad agreed. "But I doubt he's memorized that information as that would make discovering their location too easy."

While the other three waited fifty meters back, Zora tiptoed as quietly as she could to the shed. (All the curtains were drawn, meaning her approach had likely been unnoticed.)

She leaned against the wall between the door and window, closed her eyes, and began concentrating.

...

THE INTERSTELLAR DETECTIVES 3

And ten seconds later, she burst out laughing!

Her teammates realized there was no sense in being silent anymore, so they started jogging to her.

"What's so funny?" Dax inquired, wondering why Zora was still giggling uncontrollably.

"When... I..." Zora tried to say between laughs. "Read Rudd Major's mind, he was... thinking about *a mountain made of ice cream, with chocolate syrup and sprinkles raining down on it!*"

"And I took him for being the boring type," Dax laughed. "Guess I couldn't have been more wrong."

"I can hear you out there!" Rudd Major then said loudly from inside. "The coordinates you seek are in an enclosed envelope. I was not shown the coordinates, as a safeguard against what Zora just attempted. ... Now focus on your task. Put a few of the diamonds in a small bag, leave them on the doorstep, and walk 50 meters away. If you attempt to bust in, I'll burn the envelope."

(Their laughing immediately ceased... and they realized they didn't have a plan!)

"Doing that right now!" Vlad then answered (while motioning for everyone to move away from the door so they could discuss what to do.)

Dax had already pulled a small bag from his backpack and was preparing to put some of the cubic zirconia stones in it.

"Help me choose the shiniest ones," he said to his team. "And make sure they're tiny: that should trick him into thinking they're real."

"That'll never work," Vlad commented right away. "There are a bunch of super simple tests he can do to tell if they're real or fake diamonds."

"Really?" Charlotte asked. "Without any special equipment?"

"Yup," Vlad answered. "One of the easiest is the water test. Diamonds will sink in water, while fakes will float."

"I don't suppose any of you have real diamond jewelry on?" Zora then asked. "If we pried a few out from a ring or a bracelet, we could give those to him as a sample."

(But none of the four were wearing any jewelry at all, let alone something with a diamond in it!)

"I'm waiting!" Rudd Major yelled from inside. "Hurry up and bring me some samples to test!"

"Guys," Vlad said quietly to his team. "Help me think something through... Our team members were *randomly* decided upon at this morning's meeting—"

"Meaning," Zora said, continuing the train of thought, "it's highly unlikely one of our specific powers is required here."

"Which leaves only one option," Dax concluded. "We have to give a bunch of diamonds, which must be real, to Rudd Major. ... He'll test those, confirm their authenticity, and then we hand him the full suitcase of fakes in exchange for the envelope."

"But where do we get a bunch of real diamonds?" Charlotte mentioned, pointing out their plan's obvious flaw.

...

Dax then grinned.

"Did you guys all forget the lesson back at the start of Year 1?" he commented while taking his backpack off. "Hurry, pass me your laser pens."

"My laser pen?" Charlotte asked. "Why?"

Vlad picked up on what Dax was planning. "Our laser pens have some small diamonds in them," Vlad said excitedly. "I can't believe I didn't think of that earlier!"

Trying to take apart the tiny devices would have required way too much time, so Dax simply smashed all four with a hammer (and then picked the tiny diamonds out.)

"Twelve sparkly little ones, eh?" he said after finishing.

"Drop them in here," Charlotte told him, holding the small, sealable bag out.

...

Charlotte then placed the small bag in front of the cabin door, and loudly said, "We've put the bag of diamonds on the porch!"

"Wait at least 50 meters away while I open the door to grab them," Rudd Major said back. "One funny move, and the envelope goes up in flames."

...

A few minutes later—after Rudd Major has presumably tested the diamonds—the kids saw the door open a few inches.

Rudd Major stuck one arm out, envelope in hand.

"One of you," he announced loudly. "And only one of you, bring me the suitcase of diamonds. Place it on the doorstep, and I'll toss you the envelope."

(Nicely done, team!)

CHAPTER 9

The little cabin that Screed, Vivian, and Florence had been taken to by Mr. Derringer looked like nothing spectacular on the outside. (But, as explained by Mr. Derringer on the way—it was rigged up with tons of high-tech surveillance gizmos.)

After bringing the three inside, he allowed them to remove their blindfolds, and instructed them to sit on the three small wooden chairs in the middle of the otherwise furniture-free main room.

"I will not repeat what I explained before," Mr. Derringer then said while rechecking that all the equipment was functioning properly. "As soon as I walk out and close the door, the three security systems will be activated."

...

Vivian was the first to notice a digital timer on the wall, which had already begun counting and was displaying that they only had 1:43.17 left.

"This is probably just stating the obvious," Florence mentioned. "But doesn't it seem that our task might actually be to figure out how to, umm... *stop* the other team from trying to rescue us? Seeing as how the doorknob can't be touched?"

"But I can't use mind reading to communicate that fact to them when they arrive," Screed added.

"And to make things even worse," Vivian said next. "Yelling

to warn them wouldn't work; look at the walls in this room, they've been soundproofed. We'll never hear them approaching, and they'd never hear us telling them to stay back."

"Think we need to break ourselves out of here, then?" Florence pondered.

"But we'd have to get out in less than two minutes," Screed pointed out. "Because the scanner watching us will set off the bomb in two minutes once we leave this main room. ... Plus, we can't leave through the door; The doorknob would set off the bomb."

...

Soon after, Vivian realized Screed and Florence were doing the same thing she was: staring at the fireplace on the far wall (out of view of what the camera watching them was picking up.)

"This cabin has no windows," she commented. "Meaning the only other way out is the method Santa Claus uses... the chimney."

"Agreed," Screed said immediately. "But our time restraint will make that almost impossible: Remember, if the camera picks up less than three people for two minutes, then *boom.*"

"Let's take turns inspecting the chimney," Florence suggested. "Time me, Screed: tell me when it gets to ninety seconds."

...

"Ninety!" Screed yelled. "Get back over here where the camera can see you!"

"Good news," Florence told her teammates after sitting down again. "The chimney is a lot wider than I expected. ... I'm gonna go test something, time me again."

She took her chair with her.

...

"I've managed to easily get the chair inside the chimney," she said before returning. "If I were to put a second chair on top of the first one, it'd get a person high enough to climb out."

"Ninety-two!" Screed called, wanting her back immediately. "Leave the chair, but get back in camera view quickly."

...

Screed then stood up, and Florence took his chair to balance on top of the first one.

...

"I think it'll work!" she called excitedly. "But only if someone holds the top chair from sliding or toppling while the others climb out."

(But then how would the final person escape??)

In addition to that issue, they also knew they needed to get out *before* the rescue team arrived (which could potentially happen anytime...)

...

"Okay, this might sound weird," Vivian said a few minutes later, "and I don't even know if I can actually do this, but... hold on, let me try. I want you to both come here, and each sit on one of my knees."

"You are taking this Santa thing to a whole new level," Florence joked.

Once they were on her lap, Vivian closed her eyes and began concentrating. "Okay, now stand up and go way over there, out of camera view," she instructed them.

(Vivian was attempting a shapeshift she had never done before, unaware if it was even possible.)

"Oh, my," Florence exclaimed a minute later when Vivian's transformation was complete. "You just turned yourself into three people: you, me, and Screed!"
"Does it look believable?" Vivian asked, straining to hold this awkward transformation.
"Well, we are all quite a bit smaller than our normal sizes," Florence pointed out. "But other than that, looks great!"
"There's no way the sensor can detect changes in body size," Screed commented. "As far as it's concerned, there are three people in the room."
Screed was looking at his watch, waiting for the full two minutes to elapse since he and Florence had walked to where the camera couldn't see them.

...

And when that moment arrived... *no click!* (The fictitious bomb had NOT gone off.) Vivian's trick had worked!
Screed and Florence quickly walked back in camera view (so Vivian could stop this exhausting shapeshift.)
She looked a bit dazed, but was confident she'd be able to recreate and hold that shapeshift for up to ten minutes, fifteen if she pushed it.
"We'll wait till you're rested," Screed then said. "We only get one shot at this, and it's you who's doing all the work."

...

Five minutes later, Vivian told them she was *ready to roll.* On the count of three, they all stood up and dashed to the chimney.

Screed held the chairs while Florence—who could move amazingly fast because of her leg speed—climbed up.

And the instant she was out, Vivian then tightly gripped the chairs while Screed made his way up. (And since Florence was on the roof now, she'd be able to help pull Screed out once she could reach his hand.)

"Got him!" Florence yelled. "Head back and shapeshift!"

Vivian had no idea how much time was left, so she attempted to do this transformation as fast as possible.

Screed and Florence, sitting on the roof, were praying that Vivian got her shapeshift completed in time.

...

"Woohoo!" Screed cheered when his watch showed two minutes had passed since they bolted to the chimney. "I guess she switched in time!"

"Now we just have to hope the other team arrives lickety-split," Florence commented. "Before Vivian runs out of gas..."

...

"Tell you what," Florence said after examining their surroundings. "There's only one way to this cabin. I'm going to sprint down the path. Hopefully I can run into the other team on their way up."

"And what about me?" Screed asked. "What should I do?"

"You're going to talk to Vivian through the chimney," she replied. "And try to keep her calm."

"Gotcha," Screed nodded, high-fiving Florence before she jumped down from the roof. "Good luck."

CHAPTER 10

Florence's leg speed meant she could bolt down the one and only path from the cabin she'd just left at *rocket speed*. (But since it was unpaved and bumpy, she needed to be cautious not to roll an ankle.)

...

"Flo!" Vlad cheered when he spotted her running their way. (She'd only been running for slightly over a minute—but a typical person would've needed a good five minutes to cover the same distance.) "You guys busted out without our help? Nicely done!"

"Unfortunately not," she told Vlad and the others right away. "C'mon, we need you at the cabin as soon as possible. I'll explain as we run back."

...

By the time all five made it to the cabin—a little over six minutes later—they fully understood the troubling predicament Vivian was currently in.

And they could tell by Screed's expression that Vivian was not doing well—meaning her shapeshift into 3 people couldn't be held much longer.

"Guys, we need to get her out now," Screed said in a panic.

"She's overexerting herself, and she'll pass out if she holds this shapeshift any longer."

"I think I got a way to do this," Charlotte said, getting ready to transform her body into paper-thin form. "As soon as I'm thin and folded up, someone drop me down the chimney."

(Without any other suggestions, they didn't have much choice.)

...

Screed dropped the folded-up-to-the-size-of-a-notebook Charlotte down the chimney. As soon as she landed at the bottom, she reverted to her natural form and ran to Vivian.

"Viv!" she yelled to her. "You can stop the shapeshift: We're here to rescue you!"

Vivian did as instructed—reverting to her normal form. (But she was so burnt out she could barely move...)

"Start timing!" Charlotte shouted to her friends on the roof. "We've only got two minutes to do this!"

"Stay with me, girl," Charlotte then said to Vivian, helping her up.

...

"All you gotta do is climb these chairs," Charlotte told her, now in position at the bottom of the chimney. "That's Dax's arm up there: As soon as he grabs your hand, you're home free."

Vivian was shaky and somewhat disoriented, but she focused whatever energy she could muster. Hand after hand, and foot after foot, she made her way up.

...

"Got her!" Dax yelled the instant he gripped her hand. And then he used his superstrength to pull her out like she was weightless.

"Only 50 more seconds!" Vlad announced. "How do we get Charlotte out?"

(Zora, thankfully, had already figured out a way to do that!)

She was lowering a rope—to which she'd stuck the gum she had pulled out of her mouth to the end that was going down the chimney.

"Charlotte!" Zora yelled down to her. "There's gum on the end of the rope! Just—"

"I'm with 'ya!" she yelled back, aware of what Zora wanted her to do.

Charlotte grabbed the string (with the sticky wad of gum on the end), and pushed it into her hair.

"Wait 4 seconds!" she yelled up to Zora.

1, 2, 3, 4

(Charlotte had just turned into paper again.)

Zora quickly pulled (knowing *'paper Charlotte'* was stuck to the gum on the end of the string.)

"22 seconds!" Vlad—who had just jumped down from the roof—yelled. "Hurry!"

As soon as Zora had pulled Charlotte out, she slid down the side of the roof (gripping *Charlotte* in her hand.)

(Charlotte would need to wait until they got further away to revert back.)

Zora sprinted with all her might, unaware of how far she needed to be from the cabin to be safe from the impending *"fictitious"* explosion.

They all heard a voice (coming from a speaker hiding

somewhere in one of the trees) loudly say, *"Boom!"*

The kids looked back and forth at each other, waiting to hear what the voice—which they recognized immediately as being Mr. Derringer's—would say next.

"The camera we mounted in the trees," he then said through the speaker, "makes it clear that all 7 of you were more than ten meters away from the cabin when the bomb would have gone off. ... Therefore, no one would have been harmed by the blast. Congratulations, you have passed this test, with flying colors!"

"Right on!" Charlotte—having reverted to normal form now—cheered loudly, encouraging everyone to come in for a group hug. "We rock!"

"You certainly do," Mr. Derringer said through the speaker, giggling. "We'll come in two vehicles to pick you all up shortly. Oh, and since you succeeded in what we figured was virtually impossible, Ms. Morg and I will prepare the evening meal today. You all have the rest of the afternoon and evening off."

CHAPTER 11

Dinner that night ended up feeling like a celebration. Everyone (including the three adults) was in a wonderful mood, and Ms. Morg kept showering praise on the kids' amazing job today.

"We are so pleased with your quick progress," she told the Elite 7 after the meal was done, "that I personally put in a call to Headmaster Vela to brag about your accomplishments. She was ecstatic, to say the least."

"Any chance she gave us permission to skip The Academy homework?" Dax asked, smiling.

"Nice try," Ms. Morg replied, also laughing a bit. "But I'll tell you what. We are going to give you tomorrow morning off from lessons, and you can use that time to catch up on some of those assignments."

"Better than nothing, I suppose," Dax nodded.

* * *

Since they knew they could work on Academy homework the following morning, this gave them the opportunity to chill out and relax after dinner today.

Screed was so used to being perpetually busy and short of time that he didn't know what to do between now and bedtime. He was sitting on the end of his bed, joking away with Dax and Vlad, when someone knocked on their door.

"Screed, you busy?" the voice (Zora's) asked loudly through the closed door.

Vlad and Dax immediately nudged Screed, both aware that

he was waiting for an opportunity to spend time alone with Zora. Screed quickly stood up and opened the door.

Something about Zora looked a little different than usual. Screed wasn't sure if it was her clothes, her hair, her makeup (or most likely a combination of all three.)

"Do you guys mind if I steal Screed for a couple hours?" she asked, grinning.

"Go ahead," Dax replied right away. "I'm sure your company is a lot more fun than ours, anyway."

...

Since no one was wandering around in the big facility, Screed and Zora were free to go anywhere they wanted (without needing to worry about running into someone.) They began by meandering around slowly, making simple chitchat about things like today's challenge and what kind of tests might be coming next.

Screed desperately wanted to take her hand, but was way too nervous. (But at the same time, he knew she'd grow sick and tired of waiting for him to show interest... He knew he had to take some initiative, and soon.)

As they turned the corner to enter the new wing, Screed decided to *go for it*. Without looking at Zora, he reached for her hand.

"You don't think I'm scared to go in this eerily quiet place, do you?" she joked.

(Screed immediately regretted taking her hand... maybe she didn't like him enough yet!)

He forced out a laugh and went to let go of her hand. But Zora noticed this, and immediately gripped his hand tighter.

"I'm joking, silly," she smiled. Then, still clasping his hand, she twisted around to be face to face with him. "I've been waiting forever to find out if you liked me. I was starting to think I wasn't your type."

"Not my type?" Screed reacted, not sure what to say next. "You're like, you know: cute, smart, funny. You're everyone's type. You're—"

Zora could sense Screed's nervousness (and could see he was already way out of his comfort zone.)

"Since you were brave enough to make the first move," she commented, briefly looking down at their intertwined fingers. "I'll be brave next."

Then she closed her eyes, leaned in, and put her lips on his!

Screed was kissing a girl for the first time in his life! (But was he doing it right??)

CHAPTER 12

Knock-knock.

Screed, Vlad, and Dax had no idea why someone would be banging on their dorm room door well before sunrise.

"It can't be time for me to get up to prep breakfast," Vlad—who had breakfast duty in the morning—commented. "It's still pitch-black outside."

"Sorry, gentlemen," Mr. Derringer said while walking in and turning the lights on. "Something has come up, and Ms. Morg has called an emergency meeting. Quickly get dressed and come to classroom *A.*"

"This isn't another surprise test, is it?" Vlad then asked.

"Not this time," Mr. Derringer replied. "I'd love to tell you more now, but you'll all be brought up to speed shortly. ... Oh, and we've got some muffins and drinks in the classroom, just in case anyone's hungry."

...

The girls had been woken up by Ms. Morg, so they were heading to the classroom at basically the same time as the boys.

"Any clue what's going on?" Florence asked when she saw them.

"Nope," Screed answered. "Looks like they want to do this as a group announcement."

"I hope they're not sending us back to Vos early," Vlad then commented. "We haven't even been here for a week yet."

Although all seven of them were now comparing various theories about what might be going on, Ms. Morg refused to get started until everyone was seated and quiet. (Rudd Major was, of course, also here; but he appeared unaware of the nature of the upcoming news.)

"Sorry for disturbing your sleep, everyone," Ms. Morg began. "I've called this meeting because we, or perhaps it would be more accurate to say *you,* are heading out on a mission this morning."

"A mission!?" Vlad reacted. "Cool! When did The Interstellar Detective Agency contact you about this?"

"Actually," Ms. Morg replied. "This isn't a sanctioned mission request from The Agency."

The kids looked confused, as they all knew The Agency was in charge of dispatching teams to planets in peril.

"The planet Rudd Major will be flying you to is called Asos," Ms. Morg went on. "And the request from Asos' leader, President Artez, came directly to me."

"To you? Here?" Vlad inquired, wanting more details. "But—"

"Allow me to explain," Ms. Morg said, politely cutting Vlad off. "President Artez had already made three official requests to The Interstellar Detective Agency, but all three times was told her planet's issue was *not considered high priority.* And as you know, The Agency already has a huge backlog. They informed her that the likelihood of detectives being sent to help anytime soon was virtually nil."

"It just so happens," Mr. Derringer added. "That Ms. Morg and President Artez are acquaintances; They met at an Intergalactic Safety Symposium about 10 years ago, and have stayed in touch ever since."

"President Artez knows of my job here as an Elite 7 trainer," Ms. Morg said next. "And she's aware a group of trainees is here now. She called last night and asked if we could help out."

"And our school approved this?" Vlad asked right away.

"The Academy gives Mr. Derringer and I complete freedom to train you in the ways we deem best," Ms. Morg replied. "And in our opinion, a real mission offers a learning opportunity that can't be passed up."

"You're wheels up in an hour," Mr. Derringer told everyone. "Pack your stuff and grab something to eat. Ms. Morg and I will brief Rudd Major on the specifics."

CHAPTER 13

Asos was only a 4-hour flight away, so President Artez wouldn't need to wait much longer to finally get some assistance. Rudd Major was flying the Elite 7 in his ship, and Ms. Morg and Mr. Derringer were in a second ship. (Rudd Major had suggested that having two vessels was always better than one, as it meant they could split up the 7 detectives more easily if need be.)

* * *

Asos was a fairly large planet—approximately half the size of Vos—and its intriguing feature was that over 90% of the planet was covered in water.

"A sailor's paradise," Dax said while he and the others listened to Rudd Major's ship's computer explain about the planet they'd arrive at in a few hours.

…

When the computer started rattling off facts Rudd Major thought were irrelevant to their mission—such as population numbers and political groups—he gave his computer a specific instruction. "Computer," he said. "Introduce the wholphins."

(Wholphins??)

Wholphins are a species of marine life found on only a few planets in the entire galaxy. The name comes from the cross of two species—the whale and the dolphin. The wholphin is, by far, the most intelligent marine mammal documented to date. And due to that fact, wholphins are considered sacred, especially on the planet of Asos, where their numbers are plentiful. Hunting wholphins on Asos is strictly prohibited, and the wholphin population is carefully monitored by a large team of marine biologists. Every time a new wholphin calf is born, it is named and tagged. The tags are GPS trackable, allowing experts to stay up to date on their movement.

"Thank you, computer. Stop explanation," Rudd Major said. Then he spun around on his chair to face the seven kids. "The issue on Asos is regarding the wholphins. For the last few years, some concerning and shocking things have been happening: Adult wholphins have been floating up on beaches dead. And not just isolated cases here and there. Hundreds of dead wholphins. … Plus, freshly tagged baby wholphins are, somehow… disappearing."

"Have they checked the waters for new toxins?" Florence asked. "Chemical waste from factories could certainly be the culprit."

"I'm afraid I don't know that information," Rudd Major replied. "The minute we arrive on Asos, their chief marine biologist, Dr. Loft, will be meeting with us."

"Then perhaps the best thing to do now," Vlad suggested, "is to come up with a list of questions for the specialist. Guys, fire off any and all questions you can think of, and I'll jot them down."

CHAPTER 14

As their ship got closer to Asos, everyone onboard was impressed by the planet's striking beauty. The vast oceans, which covered the bulk of Asos, were a beautiful blue. And the cloud formations above various parts of the ocean looked pillowy soft.

There were only two land masses on Asos: A large one (which was in the northern hemisphere, slightly above the equator), and a smaller second one (halfway between the equator and the south pole.)

Dax—who had mentioned his love of sailing and fishing numerous times since meeting his Elite 7 teammates—was in utter awe.

"I believe I've just found my retirement spot," he commented.

"You have to start working before you can consider retiring," Charlotte joked, lightly punching his shoulder.

...

The kids looked a bit surprised when Rudd Major aimed their ship toward the smaller island.

"Apparently," Rudd Major explained, "the entire population resides on the small island. The large one is left relatively untouched, other than sites set up for mining minerals and harvesting timber."

...

After both ships had landed, they saw the welcoming party waiting to greet them.

...

And since Ms. Morg was a friend of Asos' leader, she did the introductions. "President Artez, Dr. Loft, Captain Mazden," she announced. "I'm pleased to introduce this year's Elite 7: Dax, Charlotte, Zora, Screed, Vlad, Florence, and Vivian. Oh, and their liaison, Ru—"

"Rudley, of course!" Captain Mazden (the highest-ranking marine transportation officer on Asos) said, coming to shake his hand. "I had no idea you went on to become a liaison."

"It's... Rudd Major," he said back uncomfortably.

"Well," Captain Mazden laughed. "You can call yourself whatever you want, but you are still legendary for your record streak of four victories at the Intergalactic Spacecraft Maneuvering Competition."

"The what?" Vlad asked right away.

"You've never mentioned that before, Grampa," Vivian said next.

Rudd Major looked very uncomfortable—something the kids had never seen before. "We'll discuss this later," he commented. "For now, let's stick to the mission."

...

President Artez gave them a quick tour of the facility here, which was called *Wholphin Monitoring Headquarters*. She also showed them their individual bedrooms. (The facility had over 50 individual sleeping quarters—to house their full-time staff of 20 plus any experts who came to help now and then.)

...

THE INTERSTELLAR DETECTIVES 3

Since Ms. Morg and Mr. Lexington had only come to do the introductions, they decided it was time for them to head back to Zerasta. "Please keep us posted regularly," she told Rudd Major. "And if at any point you feel this mission is becoming too risky, call it off and bring the detectives back."

"Understood," Rudd Major replied. "I'll watch over them carefully."

...

After the teens dropped their bags in their rooms, the president led them into the facility's highly secure (and guarded) main monitoring room.

"You have guards here?" Rudd Major asked the Asos leader. "Is that really necessary?"

"We didn't used to have any," she replied. "But as the wholphin situation worsened, we made the decision to increase security at our facility."

The massive room they entered had more computers and huge screens in it than the kids could ever have imagined, and there was also a big 3-D projector in the center that could be used for closer analyzations.

There were over 30 staff in here, some working alone, and some in small groups. But one thing was for sure: the atmosphere was TENSE. These experts had clearly been working 12-hour days; The bags under their eyes showed a lack of sleep.

Just as Dr. Loft got ready to outline what the various groups were each in charge of, an alarm started flashing on monitor 16—which was displaying the western-most shoreline of the large island.

"Seven adult wholphins have just washed up dead," one of the technicians announced as he got the camera mounted on that beach to zoom in closer.

"Seven!?" Dr. Loft reacted. "At this rate, the whole species will end up extinct."

"President Artez," Vlad said. "Can you fly us over there to take a look?"

"Certainly," she replied. "You might as well see firsthand; Hopefully you'll spot something we missed."

"President Artez," Captain Mazden then commented. "I'd suggest we use Rudley's, oops, I mean *Rudd Major's* ship. His vessel is at least twice as fast as any of ours."

"Agreed," the president nodded. "Rudd Major, let's go immediately. Myself, Dr. Loft, and Captain Mazden will also come aboard, if that's alright with you."

"I'd be honored," he replied.

As the group started making its way through the hallways to exit the facility, Screed noticed Captain Mazden run up beside Rudd Major, put his arm over his shoulder, and whisper something in his ear.

Rudd Major appeared to laugh, and then he held his finger in front of his lips as if he were telling Captain Mazden to keep something a secret.

(Screed immediately felt conflicted. He knew he could use his special variation of mind reading—to allow Rudd Major's thoughts in without causing a brain itch—if he wanted to, but also felt that that would be a breach of trust...)

What was Rudd Major hiding?

CHAPTER 15

Rudd Major raced his ship toward the coordinates he'd been given, and they landed a mere 23 minutes after departure. (And since the area near the beach was flat and relatively free of trees, it was easy to find a landing spot.)

"Detectives," President Artez said to the young group before giving Rudd Major the order to open the ship's door and lower the ramp. "This is not a sight for those with weak stomachs... If any of you don't feel comfortable seeing this up close, just stay on board."

Vivian quickly raised her hand. "I'll do just that, thanks," she said. "I don't think I could handle standing close to *majestical beasts* that have just died."

"And there's no need to feel embarrassed about staying," the president told her. "Back when I was your age, I couldn't even handle looking at dead goldfish."

...

"These adult wholphins are all relatively young," Dr. Loft said as they approached them. "I can't believe this is happening. They could've produced offspring for another 20 or 25 years."

"I'm sure one of you is planning to ask about this next," President Artez said, "so I might as well explain now: We have done exhaustive testing on all dead wholphins, and none have shown markers indicating a natural or artificial toxin in their system."

"And our oceans have also been inspected thoroughly," Dr. Loft added. "The water quality is pristine, just as it always has been."

"I apologize if this comment comes across as rude or insensitive," Vlad then said. "But have you ruled out foul play?"

President Artez and Dr. Loft looked at each other, extremely surprised by what this teenager was implying.

"Why would someone harm these beautiful creatures?" President Artez commented. "They are beloved by everyone on Asos."

"Then perhaps whoever is doing this is from another world?" Dax commented.

"But wholphins are peaceful, innocent creatures of the sea," Dr. Loft said. "I can't imagine a reason someone would come here to kill them."

"We aren't saying that's what's happening," Screed then said—noticing how flustered President Artez and Dr. Loft were upon hearing Vlad's theory that the wholphins were being murdered. "We're simply trying to explore all possibilities."

"Guys!" Zora—who was over by the second smallest Wholphin—yelled. "I think this one is still alive!"

Everyone rushed over, and Dr. Loft began a closer inspection.

...

"You're correct," he said. "But she's barely hanging on. She won't last much longer."

Zora then closed her eyes, and got ready to try something that shocked everyone: she was going to attempt to read the mind of this almost-dead animal!

Screed initially wanted to stop her, as he felt this could cause the dying animal to suffer unnecessary discomfort during its last minutes of life. But he elected not to say anything, partly because he wasn't in charge (and partly because he didn't want to do anything that might spoil the relationship he and Zora had recently started.)

Everyone other than Screed backed up a few paces. (Zora was focusing very hard, and they didn't want her to be distracted by anything.)

...

"Whoa!" she suddenly shouted shakily while almost losing her balance. Screed was close enough to quickly grab her and prevent what could have turned into a painful fall.

"You okay?" he asked, concerned. "What did you see?"

"That was, like," she said, appearing a bit disoriented, "so weird... and overwhelming."

"What do you mean?" he asked back.

"Well, I was moving my focus from one area of her brain to the next," she explained, "trying to lock in on recent memories. Everything was weak, likely because she's dying. But then, right after moving my focus to a new spot, I felt this... I don't know... bizarre and powerful surge of energy."

"Umm..." Screed mumbled, confused by what she was describing.

"It felt like my mind was going to explode," she told Screed. "Sorry, I can't explain it any better. It was so—"

"Odds are," Screed commented, guessing at what might have happened, "that wholphins brains are structured differently from people: That's probably why we've been taught to never attempt to use our powers on animals."

...

While Dr. Loft and most of the team moved from wholphin to wholphin, Dax was looking out to the ocean.

"Guys!" he called to everyone. "I can see two ships way out

there, maybe freighters or something? Think we should get in touch with them? Ask if they saw anything out of the ordinary?"

Captain Mazden came over and took out a pair of binoculars from his bag. "Those are ferries, actually," he explained. "They shuttle all workers and supplies back and forth between the big and small islands."

"Oh," Dax commented. "Do the ferries typically sail in twos?"

By this time, the rest of the team had come over to take a look at the far-off ferries.

"No," Captain Mazden answered. "The bigger of the two is a main ferry. The smaller one is the *emergency rescue* ferry. The big one must have had some engine trouble and called for assistance."

"I see," Dax nodded. "Well, then the captain of the big ferry would've been in this region for a while; I'd like to talk to him."

"Her," Captain Mazden said back, correcting the pronoun. "Tell you what: Let's head back to our vessel, and we can get Rudd Major to fly us over. He won't be able to land on the ferry, but we can be lowered down by ropes while hovering above it."

"Sounds good," Dax nodded.

"Ropes?" Vlad then asked, visualizing what this would entail.

"Don't be a scaredy-cat," Florence grinned, lightly elbowing him in the back. "It's not like we're bungee jumping."

CHAPTER 16

By the time Rudd Major had their ship hovering above the giant ferry, the smaller rescue ferry—no longer needed, of course—was sailing off.

Rudd Major's ship was equipped with two cables that could safely lower people down. Captain Mazden, who knew every ferry captain on the planet well, wanted to go down with the detectives to facilitate this get-together. (Dr. Loft and President Artez decided to stay with Rudd Major, so they could be easily contacted if an emergency came up somewhere else on Asos.)

There was, thankfully, very little wind, so lowering people down two by two was extremely easy. (Well, Vlad kept his eyes closed the entire time, but at least he mustered up enough courage to go!)

...

"Captain Blane," Captain Marden said once he and the detectives were on board. "Sorry about our unexpected and sudden arrival."

"No apology necessary," she smiled, shaking his hand. "Although I'm not sure how much help we can be."

Captain Mazden then took a few minutes to introduce the seven young detectives, and quickly explain how they'd just come from the shore where seven wholphins had washed up.

"Well, I'm afraid all I can tell you are facts you probably

already know," Captain Blane said, addressing the young detectives. "We were sailing our typical route and noticed a pod of wholphins in the area. As is required by protocol, we cut our engines—as we never want a wholphin to end up near a rotating propeller blade. About an hour later, when the wholphins were no longer in sight, we went to restart our engines, but couldn't."

"So you called for emergency help," Captain Mazden nodded.

"Precisely," she said. "The rescue ferry arrived quickly, sent a few technicians over to lend a hand, and within an hour, our engines were up and running again."

Captain Mazden then turned to face the detectives. "That doesn't give you much to work with, does it?" he commented, shrugging his shoulders.

Vlad had been taking notes and had already formed a few questions.

"I'm assuming you turn your engines off every time you dock to load and unload," he said to Captain Blane. "Have you had issues restarting them before?"

"Never," she replied.

"Okay," Vlad nodded, getting ready to ask his next question. "And how much time, approximately, was it between when you called for help and when they arrived?"

"Less than twenty minutes," she answered. "We were so lucky they were in the vicinity, or we would have had to wait at least a few hours."

Screed (and most of the detectives) immediately realized where Vlad was going with these questions: Those two *"highly unlikely"* events—engine failure and the unbelievably quick arrival of help—had occurred in rapid succession, which meant it was definitely more than a coincidence.

Screed needed a way to get their group some privacy (without causing Captain Blane to panic), so he asked a quick question. "Where was the person standing on the ferry when the wholphins were first spotted?" he inquired.

"The starboard," she replied. "The person who called it in was about two-thirds of the way back on the starboard side."

"Would you mind if we took ourselves there?" Screed said back. "Just want to see the exact view he saw."

"Please go anywhere you'd like," the captain smiled. "I wish I could join you, but I need to finish writing up the incident report about what happened today."

...

As soon as the detectives and Captain Mazden were distanced from all crew, Vlad outlined what they needed to do.

"We have to split up," he told them, "and *casually* investigate this without looking like we're investigating."

"You mean act like we're just touring around?" Vivian asked.

"You got it," Vlad replied. "Captain Mazden, Dax, Flo, Zora: you guys head to the engine room. Someone down there sabotaged the engines. See what you can uncover. ... Charlotte, Viv, Screed: you're with me. We're heading down to the crew's sleeping quarters."

"And what are *we* trying to do?" Charlotte asked.

"According to Captain Blane," Vlad replied. "The rescue ferry showed up unbelievably fast. I doubt its true crew are still sailing it... Someone aboard this big ferry contacted whoever is now piloting the rescue ferry the instant the wholphins were first spotted."

"Hold on," Zora commented, now following Vlad's theory. "You think the rescue ferry has been overrun by whoever is killing the wholphins... You mean, like... pirates?"

"Yes," Vlad admitted. "And since no one knows the rescue ferry is piloted by a group of imposters, they're able to sail around under the guise of *coming to help,* when what they're really doing is coming to kill wholphins."

CHAPTER 17

Captain Mazden knew the floor plan of every marine vessel ever built on Asos, so getting to the engine room was a breeze. (And having him take the three kids there would give the impression he was just giving them an *informative tour,* which wouldn't seem odd at all.)

...

The chief engineer was eager to chat with Captain Mazden, since the two were old friends from way back.

"Santos!" Captain Mazden said to his old friend. "It's been ages, hasn't it?"

"Far too long," Santos grinned while shaking hands with his old buddy. "You still rock climbing on your days off?"

"Not as much as I used to," Captain Mazden laughed. "Grip strength just isn't what it used to be."

(On their way to the engine room, Captain Mazden had told the kids that he knew the chief engineer very well—therefore theorizing it had to be one of the other engine room staff who had disabled the propulsion system.)

Their plan was simple: while Captain Mazden chatted and reminisced with Santos, Zora would try to read the minds of the other three workers down here.

***

Meanwhile, the other team of four went down to the bottom deck, where all the crew's quarters were. Vlad had come up with an intriguing plan, but implementing it was going to require some good acting skills.

"You guys ready to *put on a show?*" Vlad asked while they were in the stairwell.

"My part's easy compared to what Viv has to do," Charlotte commented.

The three Rank 2s in the group then got ready: Vlad made himself invisible, Charlotte went thin and folded herself up into a pocket-size notebook, and Vivian shapeshifted herself into Captain Blane. (And Vivian then picked up *"folded-up Charlotte"* and slid her into her pocket.)

"Alright, game on," Vlad said. (But since he was invisible, no one could see the smirk on his face!)

Vivian—who was now the spitting image of Captain Blane—strolled boldly down the hallway, talking loudly to Screed. "And here are the crew's quarters," she said (mimicking Captain Blane's voice perfectly.) "Not exactly a 5-star resort, but certainly better than some of the older ships."

While *Vivian* kept up the fake *lecture,* Vlad ran to the far end of the hallway (where the fire extinguisher was kept.) Screed and *Vivian* couldn't see him, but they could certainly see the fire extinguisher case being opened. ... Screed then gave Vlad a thumbs-up.

Vlad, as planned, aimed the fire extinguisher down the hallway and pulled the trigger to spray its high-pressure contents.

Vivian counted to 10, and then screamed, "Fire!! Fire!! All personnel, immediately vacate your rooms!!"

Doors began to open (at just about the same time Vlad dropped the almost-empty extinguisher), and everyone saw the mess of fire-retardant foam everywhere.

Screed now had an extremely challenging task to carry out,

but he was fairly confident he could do it. (The theory they were going with was as follows: Whoever was communicating with *the bad guys running the rescue ship* must have a special device for those communications in his or her room. And upon being suddenly ordered out of their rooms, that person would likely hide the device in a hard-to-find spot before exiting—aware that a post-fire safety check would be performed in each room.)

Screed opened his mind, and allowed the thoughts of all those on this floor in… He didn't *focus* on any specific person's thoughts; He simply let them all *brush through* his mind. (He was waiting to sense some type of *'I've gotta hide the communicator!'* panic from someone.)

…

And it did!

"It's one of the rooms on the left, somewhere behind us," he said softly to *Vivian.* "But I'm not sure exactly which one; I could only get the approximate location." (For the past few months, Screed had been practicing hard to pinpoint "where" certain thoughts were coming from. He had improved his ability to decipher the direction relative to his position where a thought had emerged, but he currently couldn't be much more accurate than that.)

Vivian and Screed quickly went to that part of the hallway. Two of the three rooms' doors were open (and the two crew members were standing at their open doors awaiting further instructions), but one door was still closed…

Vivian banged on that door. "Open up immediately!" she screamed. "There's been a fire down here!"

Screed nodded to *Vivian:* indicating he had sensed that the person they were after was behind this closed door.

The door then opened, and the nervous-looking crew member apologized for taking so long, claiming he had been *sleeping like a rock.*

"You were the last one to react!" *Vivian* scolded him, taking a few steps into the room.

"I'm sorry, Captain," the young man replied. "I sleep with earplugs in."

"You slept during all this commotion!?" *Vivian* asked loudly, encouraging the young man to look out into the hallway.

(And while he did that, she surreptitiously took Charlotte out of her pocket and dropped her on the floor under the desk!)

"All crew!" *Vivian* yelled powerfully. "Move down to the far end of the hall where the fire extinguisher is."

A ship's crew knew to never question its captain's orders, so they all treaded through the mess of fire retardant to the end of the hall.

(And that meant Charlotte could revert to her usual form and rapidly search for the hidden communicator.)

"If I had to hide something very quickly," she mumbled to herself, eyes darting around the small room. "Where would I put it?"

(The clock was ticking, as Charlotte knew *Vivian* could only keep the crew down at the far end of the hallway for a limited amount of time.)

Charlotte couldn't, of course, rapidly and messily go through the drawers and closet. She needed to make sure that nothing looked like it had been touched when she was done in here.

"He wouldn't have put it in a drawer," she pondered. "And his closet is almost bare… Plus, the bed would be a dangerous option, since whoever does housekeeping might discover it while taking the sheets off to wash them."

Charlotte then looked toward the room's open door... and grinned. (She assumed that crew here, similar to military personnel, were expected to always keep their things neat and perfectly lined up.)

"His work boots," she commented, walking over to them, "certainly aren't placed neatly in a pair. ... One of them, in fact, is lying on its side."

She squatted down and slid her hand into the toppled-over (and fairly stinky) boot. ... And sure enough, there was a small device inside it!

"Bingo," she said softly to herself, carefully pulling it out. She then quickly opened the flap where the battery was kept, and inserted a flea-sized tracker: that would allow them to intercept all future communications on this frequency.

She then took out her own communicator, and entered a command to make everyone on her team's communicators vibrate 3 times: to signal *"mission accomplished!"*

(This also meant it was time for Vlad to do his next task.)

Vlad had climbed up the stairwell just beside where he had used the fire extinguisher. He'd gone visible again (but no one could see him because he was at the top of the stairwell.) And he had removed a fire extinguisher from the next floor up.

But instead of pulling the trigger, he intentionally dropped this one, and let it noisily bang and bounce down the stairs.

"Go see who did that! Hurry!" *Vivian* ordered everyone.

As the crew ran up that far stairwell, Charlotte left the small room and exited this floor via the other staircase.

"Captain! One of those teenagers is fooling around with fire extinguishers!" a crew member called to *Vivian* as soon as he saw Vlad—looking extremely guilty—at the top of the stairs.

"Bring him to me, now!" she ordered the crew. "But don't harm him: Just walk him down."

Vlad did his best to force out some fake crying. "I'm sorry," he pleaded, sobbing. "I just, like, always wanted to be a firefighter, and I—"

"Where exactly was the fire!?" *Vivian* loudly questioned him.

"Um... there wasn't one, I'm sorry," he whimpered. "I just wanted to use a fire extinguisher. I had never—"

"Silence!" Vivian screamed. She then strongly grabbed Vlad's wrist. "I'm escorting you and your team off this ship. And I'll also be lodging an official complaint to the government. This is outrageous."

Vivian then addressed the crew. "Looks like this was all about nothing," she told them. "You may return to your rooms. After I've watched these misbehaving immature brats leave our ship, I'll assign a cleanup team to take care of this mess."

...

As *Vivian* stormed down the hallway—with Vlad by the wrist and Screed following closely behind—Charlotte, who had heard the commotion from where she was hiding in the nearby stairwell, sent a message to the team members in the engine room.

> *Go to the upper deck as fast as you can: We must return to Rudd Major's ship immediately.*

* * *

The other group, which had yet to find who the "mole" was, quickly stopped their investigation and started heading up—back where they'd been dropped off by Rudd Major.

(They needed to get off this ship before someone informed *the real Captain Blane* of what had happened!)

...

When everyone had arrived at the pick-up spot (with Rudd Major's ship now hovering just overhead), they were relieved that no crew were in sight. Vivian then reverted to her normal form, and Rudd Major—who had lowered the two cables the instant he saw them arrive—got ready to bring the first two people back up.

Captain Blane—who had yet to hear of the *shenanigans*—could see that Rudd Major was hoisting people up by cable (because there were windows on all 360 degrees of the helm room.) She wanted to inquire about this right away, but it would take her a few minutes to get from the helm to where they were.

...

Captain Mazden and Screed, the final two still on the ferry, were just strapping the cables on when Captain Blane arrived.

"Captain Blane," Captain Mazden said right away, preparing to cook up a lie. "An emergency has come up elsewhere, and President Artez ordered us back to the ship."

"Ah," Captain Blane replied, seeming to understand (and believe) the reason behind the urgency. "Well, if you have any questions, feel free to contact me anytime."

...

With all eight safely back aboard Rudd Major's ship again, Captain Mazden turned to face Vlad.

"I suppose whatever you did down there," he commented, "is going to turn into a lot of questions coming from Captain Blane?"

"Highly likely," Vlad admitted, giggling a bit. "Our method was a little unorthodox, but it did get the job done."

"A little unorthodox??" Vivian laughed. "That's the biggest understatement I've ever heard!"

CHAPTER 18

"Great job, everyone," Rudd Major said, commending the team as he flew away from the big ferry. "That little device Charlotte installed is effectively hooked into the frequency the bad guys are using to communicate with each other."

"And I'd be willing to bet," Captain Mazden commented, "that every ferry has been infiltrated by a few of those bad guys. The next time any one of them sends a message to the hijacked rescue ferry about a wholphin spotting, we'll be listening."

"And that means we can get there first," Screed smiled, "set up a sting operation, and get to the bottom of this."

The Elite 7 members sat in a circle on the floor and began hashing out a plan. They wanted to come up with one as quickly as possible, as they had no idea when the next wholphin sighting would occur...

"In the meantime," Rudd Major asked the teens. "Where should I take us? Back to Wholphin Monitoring Headquarters?"

"That'd put us too far away from where the bulk of the ferries are," Vlad pointed out. "I'd say our best bet is to stay airborne, and keep ourselves halfway between the large and small islands: then we'll be within a reasonable distance of everything in the water."

"Understood," Rudd Major replied. "With Captain Mazden's help, we'll to pick suitable coordinates to hover."

* * *

After about half an hour of waiting (and wondering how long

before they'd intercept a communication…), Vlad came up with an *alternative:* one that would allow them to act now instead of later.

"Captain Mazden," Vlad asked the head of Asos' marine fleet. "I'm assuming there's a way of figuring out the hijacked rescue ferry's current location?"

"Indeed, there is," he replied. "Give me a few minutes, and I'll get those coordinates for you."

"And Rudd Major," Vlad asked their liaison next. "We've got a few inflatable rafts, right?"

"Of course," he answered. "Vostian ships are required to have three on board at all times, in case an engine issue was to happen while over a body of water."

"And we've also got things like emergency flares?" Vlad asked next.

"Oh yes," Rudd Major replied, nodding. "I think I have an inkling of what you're about to suggest."

…

After explaining this new idea to everyone and getting the coordinates (and sailing path) of the rescue ferry, Rudd Major had them on their way there.

They were heading for a spot in the ocean a few kilometers ahead of the rescue ferry's path. But before approaching that spot, Rudd Major turned on his ship's stealth mode.

…

He took his ship down so it was a few meters above the ocean surface. The waves looked relatively gentle, which would make this a bit easier.

"Our ship is cloaked," Screed commented, a bit worried. "But the rafts we are about to lower certainly aren't. Doesn't that put us at risk of being spotted while dropping them into the ocean?"

"We are far away from the rescue ferry," Rudd Major explained. "There's no way they'll notice. From where they are, our floating rafts would look smaller than ants."

They'd done the raft inflating during the flight to these coordinates, so all they needed to do was lower two rafts (using the cables), and then lower the 7 teens and Dr. Loft. (President Artez and Captain Mazden were too well-known, so they couldn't participate in this operation.)

...

Once all eight were safely lowered to the two rafts, Rudd Major took his ship to a higher altitude (but stayed in stealth mode, just to be safe.)

"Everyone clear on our cover story?" Vlad repeated loudly so everyone on his raft and the other could hear.

"I'm Mr. Bastilia, and you're my pupils," Dr. Loft said, repeating the tale Vlad had just told him to memorize. "We were out doing some ocean testing as part of a school project when a strong current took us off course. And we've run out of fuel, so we're just floating aimlessly."

"Perfect," Vlad nodded. "Rudd Major emptied the motors' gasoline tanks before lowering the rafts, so the ferry crew will have no reason to think we're lying."

"Plus," Screed added. "We brought along lots of test tubes and other chemistry stuff—to make our story look believable."

...

"Alright, time to use the flares," Vlad announced when the ferry was roughly a kilometer away.

These flares didn't shoot in the air; They were more like sticks that constantly spewed out brightly-colored fire. Two people in each raft were using one so these bright flares would be impossible for the crew aboard the rescue ferry to miss.

...

Since those who had hijacked the rescue ferry needed to keep up the facade that they were real Asos marine vessel employees, there was no way they could ignore the SOS from the stranded rafts.

The ferry flashed its headlights and sounded its horn: signaling they'd seen the rafts and would pull up beside them.

"Alight, Vlad," Screed said to his best friend. "Time for you to go invisible."

"Yup," he smiled. "They'll think there are only seven of us, leaving me free to secretly roam around the ship."

...

When the rescue ferry pulled up beside them about 10 minutes later, two of the ship's crew and the captain (who Screed and his team assumed were all imposters) were waiting at the top of the ladder mounted on the ship's side.

"Climb up one at a time!" the captain shouted down. "Put whatever supplies you need to keep in your backpacks!"

"Understood!" Dr. Loft shouted back. "My pupils and I are so relieved—we've been floating out here, gasless, for over 3 hours!"

Screed went up first (and Vlad—invisible—was right behind him.) Immediately after being helped onto the deck by the two crew, Screed took a couple of steps forward—to allow Vlad some space to get himself on the deck.

About twenty seconds later, Screed felt two light taps on his shoulder. (Vlad was safely on the ferry!)

...

With the entire team safely aboard now, the two crew descended the ladder and hooked up the rafts to cables so they could hoist them up as well.

"My name is Reginald Bastilia," Dr. Loft lied, putting his hand out to greet the captain. "Would you mind lending us your ship's radio? I need to contact the school and the authorities, to explain what happened."

"Follow me," the captain—not happy at all about these guests—said without even giving his name. "But there's no need for your students to come to the helm. ... I'll have my men lead them to the kitchen: I'm sure they must be starving."

...

Two more crew members—also imposters, no doubt—were in charge of guiding the teens to the kitchen. They were equally unfriendly: likely viewing this group's sudden appearance as a major inconvenience.

"Feel free to help yourself to anything in the fridge, freezer, or cabinets," one of the two said expressionlessly. "All we ask is that you wash up after yourselves: there are no official kitchen staff on this ferry."

"We'll leave it spotless," Charlotte assured the unhappy crew.

"And while aboard," the other crew member said, "you're restricted to the kitchen, and your sleeping quarters—which we will take you to after you've eaten."

(That, of course, was an overly strict rule... But the team knew not to push their luck by questioning it.)

"As guests on your ship," Charlotte smiled, "we'll obey everything you say. ... But if we need something, let's say for a medical purpose, how can we get in touch with someone?"

"There's a phone on the wall over there," he replied, pointing to the kitchen's entrance. "Dial 12, and you'll be connected to the helm."

The two crew then went to leave. "When you're ready to be

shown to your rooms," one said, "call the helm."... And then they both coldly walked out.

Zora knew Screed had had his mind open to pick up the crew members' thoughts, so she immediately inquired as to what he had learned.

"Unfortunately," Screed told her and the others. "Their thoughts didn't reveal much. ... But they were both terrified of what punishment they might receive if we were to go anywhere else on the ship."

"Well, first things first," Dax then said. "Let's eat, clean up, and do everything else they're expecting. The less suspicious they get, the better."

"And while we chow down," Florence smiled, "we can start forming our plan of attack; We can't leave all the investigating to Vlad, that's too much pressure on him."

"Agreed," Screed said, extremely worried about his best friend.

CHAPTER 19

Since Vlad now had over two full years of using his power, he was easily able to keep himself invisible for extended periods of time—hours on end, if necessary—without even breaking a sweat.

The biggest challenge Vlad found himself facing while moving around the ship was opening doors. (Doors were simple to open, of course; The problem was that if he opened one and someone was behind it, they would immediately wonder how/why the door suddenly opened.) And simply waiting and waiting for someone else to open it—which would allow him to sneak through behind whoever opened the door—could mean waiting forever...

The best scheme he came up with was this: First, go through the hallways and make notes of specific rooms he felt were worth investigating. Next, go up and *"knock once"* on a door he wanted to look behind, and wait to see if someone came to open it. (If someone did open it, he might be able to slip in; And if no one came, then it was likely no one was inside, meaning he could do the opening himself.)

...

The biggest of the three rooms he wanted to inspect was way at the back of the ferry (and presumably used for storage.) After ensuring no one was near him, Vlad—still invisible, of course—went up to the door and knocked once.

...

No one came to the door. (That meant he could go in on his own!)

As he had guessed, this was a supplies storage area. (But the type of supplies in here made Vlad very uneasy as these things certainly weren't being used for assisting stranded ferries with engine troubles...)

The supplies were sorted, clean, and very organized. On a table in the corner was a pile of massive *needles*—similar to what a doctor might use to draw blood from someone's arm—but they had the diameter of a garden hose and were at least 12 inches long. And on the floor next to those were tons of rolled-up hoses, which obviously could be attached to the non-sharp end of the fat needles.

There were also piles of harpoon-like devices, which Vlad assumed were for shooting the wholphins.

The biggest mystery in here was what Vlad uncovered when he opened up a large refrigerator: There were many big glass vials, each of which could probably hold a liter or so of contents. Vlad didn't bother counting them, but at first glance there appeared to be at least thirty. And each one had a hand-written label on it, which simply showed a date—presumably the date each was filled.

And he quickly realized the seven vials on the fridge's top shelf were labeled with the exact date he and his team had seen the seven freshly killed wholphins shortly after landing on Asos.

It was pretty easy for Vlad to surmise that the contents of these containers came from some part of the wholphins (by using the big needles and tubes to *suck it out.)*

"I wonder what this stuff is?" Vlad asked himself, holding one container in his hand while inspecting its color and consistency. "It's got blood mixed in with it, but the bulk of it appears more like a greyish, thick mush."

Vlad quickly took off his backpack and removed a sealable,

shatter-resistant test tube. "I'll take a sample back with me," he commented while using a Pasteur pipette (basically an eye dropper) to suck some of the mush out and then put it in the test tube. "Rudd Major's ship has a device that can tell us exactly what this stuff is."

Vlad then put the test tube into his backpack and got ready to leave the room.

…

But before he got to the door, it suddenly opened and two crew members walked in! (Luckily, Vlad had gone invisible a few seconds earlier…)

"Captain wants us to reconfirm the container count," one of the crew said to the other. "Another rendezvous will be set up if we have enough."

"Gotcha," the other (slightly younger) man commented while opening the fridge.

After counting and recounting, which confirmed they had 43 full glass containers, the two got ready to exit.

(Vlad figured the safest option was to let both leave first and then exit on his own a few minutes later.)

But once the crew had left and shut the door, Vlad heard the click of a lock!

"Captain asked me to keep this room locked," Vlad heard one of the crew members comment from the hallway. "Just in case our guests accidentally find their way down here."

Oh no! This was bad… (This door's lock was keyed on both sides… Vlad was trapped!)

CHAPTER 20

The rest of the Elite 7 felt their communicators vibrate: this was likely a message from either Rudd Major or Vlad.

"Drat," Screed said when he read Vlad's message. "Guys, we need to go get him."

"But we're restricted to our sleeping quarters and the kitchen," Vivian reminded Screed. "If anyone sees us roaming the ship, they'll immediately stop us and report it to the captain."

"She's right," Dr. Loft commented. "Vlad's currently not in danger. Perhaps it's best if we wait."

"Not an option," Screed said back right away. "We are busting him out right now."

"Well," Dax mentioned. "I definitely need to be part of this rescue: I can use my arm strength to rip the door open in a flash."

"So, all we need to do," Screed said, "is find a way to get Dax there and back without being spotted."

They toyed around with a few different suggestions, but nothing struck them as being *foolproof* or *ideal*. (And the longer they discussed this, the longer Vlad had to wait...)

Dr. Loft—who had simply just listened as the clever teens suggested options—unexpectedly offered up an idea. "Now I know I'm not a detective by any stretch of the word," he said. "But I would say the best way to allow Dax a path to the back of the ship unseen is to get the entire crew to go to the front first."

"That does make sense," Charlotte nodded. "But how can we get the WHOLE crew to dash up there at the same time?"

...

"I have an idea," Screed then said, "although doing so may end up getting me expelled from The Academy."

"You're not going to use your powers to—" Zora started to ask.

"I have no choice," Screed told her, shrugging his shoulders. "I just hope I can do it properly..."

Dr. Loft picked up the phone in the kitchen, dialed the number the crew had told them before, and said one of his pupils needed to use the ship's communication system to contact his doctor... (He said that this child takes medicine for migraine headaches, but didn't bring any with him because it was supposed to be a short day. The pupil therefore needed to ask his doctor how to treat the migraine that had started coming on a few minutes ago.)

...

Dr. Loft and Screed walked themselves to the bridge after being given the okay by the captain (who was growing more and more irritated by the guests' presence on board.)

...

"We appreciate your help," Dr. Loft said to the captain as he and Screed (who was acting very unwell) entered the helm. "I'll have to call this young man's doctor on his behalf; his head hurts too much to do so himself."

The captain didn't reply; He simply pointed toward the communication panel and then told one of the crew to assist.

Dr. Loft helped Screed over to a chair, and then put a black cloth over the boy's head. "The darker his surroundings, the better," he told the crew before heading to the communicator. "He told me that light intensifies the pain."

(The cloth was thin enough that Screed could see through it: meaning he knew the precise location of everyone in the room.)

Dr. Loft dialed the number for his own doctor, knowing the bad guys running the ship would be satisfied when a doctor's receptionist picked up the call.

...

"Hailey's Medical Clinic," a voice said after answering. "Linda speaking. How may I help you?"

The captain nodded to the crew member manning the communicator, signaling that the rest of the call didn't need to be on the intercom.

As Dr. Loft started explaining to the receptionist about the emergency his pupil was having, Screed got ready to *work his magic*. He was only going to get one shot at this, and he couldn't blow it...

(Although Screed was aware of *how* to do the technique he was about to attempt, he had never actually tried it before.)

Screed—through the thin, black cloth draped over his face—double-checked the current location of the captain. He then took a few deep breaths and got ready to focus.

...

About ten seconds later, the captain—looking suddenly uncomfortable and unwell—grabbed a pole for support.

"Are you okay, sir?" one of the crew asked him.

The captain didn't reply at first...

The captain then took a seat, put his hands on his head, and said, "My skull is pounding. ... I can't even think."

The crew looked confused.

"You mean you have a headache, sir?" one asked.

"A brutal headache!" he snapped back. "And it came on out of nowhere!"

Dr. Loft knew he needed to say something to get the crew to worry even more.

"That's exactly what my pupil said about fifteen minutes ago," he told everyone.

Screed then got ready to ramp up the painful, stabbing headache he was giving the captain.

"Aarrgh!" the captain wailed, falling to the floor. "This is unbearable!"

(And then the captain passed out from the pain!)

One of the crew—presumably the second-in-command, got on the ship's main speaker.

"All hands! To the helm immediately!" he yelled into the intercom. "The captain's had an accident!"

* * *

Since that message had been blared through every speaker on the entire ship, the Elite 7 members who were still in the kitchen heard it as well.

"Screed sure is good," Zora smiled. "Inflicting pain is one of the most challenging mind reader skills."

"How long should I wait before heading to get Vlad?" Dax—hand on the doorknob—asked eagerly.

"Maybe another two minutes or so," Charlotte advised. "Just to be safe. The last thing we want is for a crew member running to the helm to see you."

...

After counting to 120, Dax opened the door, saluted his team, and started dashing to where Vlad was trapped.

* * *

When he got to the locked storage room, the first thing he did (which was something Vivian had suggested) was slide a piece of paper under the door, which read:

I'm busting you out! Stand back from the door!

(He technically could have yelled it through the locked door, but figured this non-verbal option was the safest—just in case a random crew member happened to be in the vicinity.)

...

If Dax had had more time (and the appropriate tools), picking the lock might have been possible. But since he had neither, his only choice was to open it by brute force.

He put his "strong" hard on the locked handle, and twisted until he heard a snap (of the locking mechanism breaking.)

Then he opened the door, and saw Vlad waiting a few feet back, grinning.

"Thanks, dude," Vlad said.

"My pleasure," Dax replied, standing aside so Vlad could walk out. "But you had better go invisible again. Remember, there are only supposed to be six teenagers here."

Before doing that, Vlad inspected the damage done to the lock. He fiddled with the doorknob, wondering how well it still worked...

"Well, the lock mechanism is toast," he told Dax. "But at least the handle still twists. If we're lucky, whoever comes here next will just assume it wasn't locked."

"But what if the guys who locked it are the ones who come

here next?" Dax asked.

"Then we're in trouble," Vlad gulped, preparing to go invisible again. ... "Alright, you lead the way; I'll follow right behind."

"Gotcha," Dax nodded, heading back along the same route he'd used to get here.

CHAPTER 21

Screed knew he could now stop inflicting pain into the captain's mind, but decided to *dampen it in stages* over the next 30 or 40 seconds (instead of abruptly stopping.)

First, he cut the headache part in half, and added some ear ringing ('tinnitus' in medical terms.) ... And about fifteen seconds after that, he stopped the headache entirely, and added some lightheadedness and vertigo. ... And finally, he let everything fade away.

"Captain," the second-in-command, now panicking, said. "Can you see me? Do you know where you are? Can you—?"

"I'm fine," the captain replied while slowly getting ready to stand up. "Now help me into my seat."

Dripping in sweat from the strain he had put on himself to give the captain a headache (but face still effectively hidden by the black cloth), Screed made sure not to do anything to draw attention to himself. He forced himself to take slow, deep breaths, hoping that would slow his racing heartbeat.

"Is there a doctor on board?" Dr. Loft asked. "Someone who can take a look at my pupil and the captain? It seems they are suffering from something very similar."

"I told you, I'm fine," the stubborn captain replied coldly. "And no, we have no physicians, or anyone with medical training, on board."

Dr. Loft knew what was required next: to get himself and Screed out of the helm and back to the kitchen.

"I'm going to take this young man to his room so he can lie down," Dr. Loft said while helping Screed up. (And he left the black cloth in place, so Screed wouldn't have to fake a facial expression while leaving.)

* * *

Vlad and Dax were now back in the kitchen, and while waiting for Dr. Loft and Screed to return, were working with the other Elite 7 members to hash out a plan.

"We've gotta get this sample to Rudd Major's ship ASAP," Charlotte said, stating her opinion.

"I completely agree," Vlad nodded. "But how? We can't relaunch one of our rafts; It'd take too long, plus they'd see us doing so and stop us in the act."

...

"We've all got waterproof GPS monitors on our belts," Dax said a minute later, smiling... "Vlad, you can swim, right?"

"Um... yes," he replied. "But I can't jump overboard and then contact Rudd Major to pick me up, if that's what you're suggesting. There's a chance I'd get sucked against the ship and then shredded by the propellers."

"Perhaps you're forgetting something," Dax winked. "I have one fast arm and one strong one. ... So, we go to the side of the ship, you become invisible, and then I grab your arm with both of my hands; With my strength and speed powers working in sync, I can toss you further than a pro baseball player throwing from right field to home plate."

Vlad had no option other than to agree. But before going, he needed to send a couple of the remaining Elite 7 members to investigate the one room he knew needed checking.

"Guys, there's a room," Vlad said, speaking quickly, "way deep in the bowels of the ship and near the front, that has to be investigated. I was going check it out myself, but those losers locked me in before I had a chance."

"Viv and I will go," Charlotte suggested right away. "If we hear anyone coming while making our way there, I can turn into paper and she can transform herself into one of the crew."

"But what if the door's locked?" Zora commented. "Which is pretty likely, considering we know they're trying to hide things from us."

"Then I'd better go, too," Dax said.

"But you're heading up to toss Vlad into the water," Florence mentioned.

"The instant I fling him," Dax said while getting to leave with Vlad, "I'll bolt down to that room."

"Okay, but be careful," Charlotte said before the two boys left. … "Alright, see you down there shortly."

Vivian and Charlotte also got ready to go, which was going to leave only Zora and Florence behind (until Screed and Dr. Loft returned.)

"We'll update Rudd Major on what's happening," Florence said, "so that he knows to be ready for Vlad. Plus, if any crew members come here, we'll tell them the rest of you are napping in your quarters."

CHAPTER 22

Knowing how much each second counted, Vlad and Dax sprinted to an appropriate spot for Dax to *fling his teammate* into the ocean.

...

Dax made sure his footing was sound, and then he tightly gripped Vlad's left wrist with both hands.

"Please don't dislocate my shoulder while doing this," Vlad gulped.

"Don't worry," Dax winked. "But if I accidentally do, Rudd Major knows first aid and he'll pop it back in in a jiffy."

Vlad then went invisible—to ensure none of the crew (all assumably still in the helm) would see him being a *human cannonball*.

...

"Okay, I'll do it on the count of three," Dax then said. "One, two, three!"

And Vlad—invisible to everyone (Dax included)—went soaring through the air.

Dax didn't even stick around to watch the splash when his friend landed because he needed to get to the bottom level of the ferry before any crew began moving about again.

* * *

When he made it to the door where Vivian and Charlotte were waiting for him, both girls let out a sigh of relief.

"Good thing you're here," Vivian commented. "Zora was right: it's locked."

"Hey Dax," Charlotte said as he got ready to bust the lock. "Did you notice the ferry suddenly change direction and accelerate a minute ago?"

"I was bolting through hallways and down stairwells," he told her. "I didn't feel a thing."

"Well, the captain is heading somewhere in a hurry," Charlotte explained. "The ship's on full throttle."

...

Just like when he had busted Vlad out of the supply room, Dax effortlessly twisted the locked handle until they heard the *snap* of the lock breaking.

"Ladies first," Dax then said while winking at Charlotte.

She blushed a bit, and then walked in. Vivian and Dax followed directly behind, and Dax then closed the door.

"What the...?" Charlotte said, confused by what she was looking at. "Why would they install a huge window on the bow of a ship, below the waterline?"

"It looks like this part of the ship has been built with clear, thick plastic," Vivian commented after walking up to it. "I feel like I'm in an aquarium: being able to look at the sea through a window."

There were four chairs in the room—which were all welded to the floor to prevent them from sliding around when the ship bobbed or rolled.

"They even have front-row seats for people to watch the marine life while relaxing," Dax joked while sitting down on one of them. (But due to the ferry's current high speed, there wasn't much to look out at through the window other than seawater.)

Both sides of this room were lined with a mess of boxes and large crates. The three detectives were hopeful that inspecting the contents of a few would help provide a clue as to what went on in here.

...

"This one's just filled with non-perishables," Dax told his teammates. "Canned fish, canned fruit, things like that."

"And this one's cleaning supplies," Vivian said next. "Nothing odd or weird about that."

...

As they continued checking things, they realized the ferry had slowed to a crawl.

"I guess we've arrived wherever the ship was heading," Charlotte commented.

"Well, it certainly wasn't to a land mass," Vivian—now standing over by the big window—said. "Nothing but ocean out there."

"I say we head back to the kitchen," Dax then suggested. "Other than the weird window and four seats, this room is pretty boring: it's just a place for overstock."

As they got ready to reopen the door, they heard footsteps and voices coming down the hallway.

"This is not good," Dax whispered in a panic. "We can't leave right now. We gotta find somewhere to hide, and quickly."

Thankfully, there was an area on the left side of the room where the crates were stacked on top of each other: allowing a convenient spot to squat down (to remain unseen.)

* * *

Since Rudd Major was keeping his vessel cloaked (and Vlad was currently invisible), the ferry crew had no way of seeing him being pulled out of the water via a cable.

...

"Vlad, you alright?" Rudd Major asked Vlad the second he pulled him aboard. "And turn off your invisibility; we need to make sure you don't have any wounds that need attending."

"Oops, almost forgot I was invisible," Vlad commented while shutting his powers off. "We'll have to save my health inspection for later; We have to scan a sample I stole from the ferry."

...

"What... is this?" President Artez asked after looking at the goopy mess in the sealed vial.

"It was extracted from some part of a wholphin," Vlad answered. "We need to learn which part as that will hopefully help us figure out why they are doing this and who might be behind it."

Rudd Major handed the ship controls over to Captain Mazden (who could pilot airborne vessels in addition to marine ones), and then took the vial to the analyzer. "It'll take anywhere from a few minutes to a few hours," he explained. "All we can do is wait."

While Rudd Major double-checked the analyzer's settings, Captain Mazden steered them in the direction that the rescue ferry had gone.

"And by the way," Rudd Major said next. "The device Charlotte slipped into that radio allowed us to overhear a recent call. Another ship, fairly close by, has spotted a mother wholphin and her calf. Odds are that's where the rescue ferry's going."

"We'll get there shortly," Captain Mazden announced. "And that'll let us see firsthand what happens."

"What's worrying me right now," Vlad then commented, "is figuring out how to get the Elite 7 and Dr. Loft off the ferry. The longer we leave them down there, the riskier their situation gets."

"We'll cross that bridge when we come to it," Rudd Major told Vlad while patting him on the back. "And don't worry, I've got a few tricks up my sleeve. ... Plus, we still need to learn about what Charlotte, Vivian, and Dax find in the room near the bow."

...

Ping.

"What was that?" Vlad asked, looking around. "I hope that isn't your vessel telling us there's a problem with the cloak."

"Nope," Rudd Major grinned. "That's the analyzer telling us the sample testing is complete."

Vlad and Rudd Major walked over to read the data being displayed on the analyzer's screen.

"This is, um..." Rudd Major said, briefly pausing because what he was seeing on the screen was extremely disturbing. "Unfathomable..." He then turned around to address the president and Captain Mazden. "According to the scan, 94% of the vial's contents are wholphin brain matter, specifically from the cerebrum's parietal lobe."

The president's face turned blue; The criminals on the rescue ferry were sucking portions of wholphins' brains: Not only was that murder, but it was also grotesque and brutal.

"What could they possibly want wholphin brain for?" Vlad asked. "Does it have some sort of healing property? Is it used as medicine?"

"Not that I know of," the president replied.

"President Artez," Vlad said to Asos' visibly shaken leader. "I'm extremely sorry for what's going on. ... But I assure you, we'll get to the bottom of this. The crew of crooks in that ferry are periodically handing over the extracted brain matter to whoever they work for."

"I like Vlad's way of thinking," Rudd Major nodded. "We'll stick close by the ferry, and wait for the next rendezvous—"

"And then follow them," Vlad mentioned, "to see who's buying it and what it's being used for."

CHAPTER 23

Through a gap between two of the crates they were hiding behind, Dax had a fairly good view of the small group of people who had just come in and sat down on the seats in front of the big window. (And the fact that the "mysterious captain" was one of those in here meant it must be for something very important.)

"Captain," one of the crew said as they sat at the only four seats in here (which all faced the giant window.) "Are you positive you heard the orders correctly?"

"I asked them to repeat the order, just to be sure," the captain replied. "To be honest, I am just as surprised as you are. Up till now, we've always killed the mothers when kidnapping their calves."

Dax shifted his focus to the window (as he had noticed some movement out there.)

Quite far off, he saw a majestic wholphin adult-baby pair. The baby, likely dependent on its mother for safety and comfort, stayed glued to her.

And just outside the big window, a team of four divers (in scuba gear) was descending. Each was holding a corner of a giant square net, which Dax guessed would be used for trapping and then lifting the wholphins out of the ocean.

"They've told us to kidnap the mother as well this time," the captain said loudly into a device that allowed him to speak to the divers. "You can stun her a bit to slow her movement, but she must remain alive."

One of the divers gave a thumbs-up sign, indicating he'd heard the captain's instructions clearly.

"Why do they want the mom?" the crew member to the captain's right asked. "I thought it was only the babies they were experimenting on."

"It is," the captain replied. "But many of the babies have died soon after being kidnapped, most likely because of the mental toll from being pulled away from their mothers."

"Ah," the crew member nodded. "So, taking the mom should keep this calf happy and healthy—"

"Meaning they can perform more experiments for much longer times," the captain added.

"But does their transport vessel have a tank big enough for both?" another member of the crew asked.

"Apparently so," the captain replied. "They recently swapped in a much bigger tank—specifically to allow this to be possible."

...

The captain and crew watched eagerly as the team of trained divers used various techniques to lure the wholphins closer to their net. (Their coordinated efforts and timing showed that they had done this many times in the past.)

...

A fifth crew member then entered the room to give the captain an update. "The transport vessel is flying our way now," he said. "They'll be above us within the next 15 or 20 minutes."

"Perfect," the captain smiled. "We should have the wholphins netted and ready to lift by then."

...

Charlotte was rapidly tapping Dax's shoulder. He twisted his head to see what she wanted, and saw that she was pointing to the room's door—which had been left open by the person who had just walked in.

Dax nodded, understanding that they now had a chance to get out without being spotted.

There was only a narrow gap between the crates and the side wall, so Vivian—who was the closest to the door—led the way.

...

They easily slipped out unnoticed, aided by the fact that the five crew in the room were hyper-focused on the divers and wholphins.

There was only one hallway down here, which led to a single, narrow stairwell that would take them up. In silence, while also trying to step lightly enough for their footsteps to make no noise, they made their way to the stairwell.

"Oh, no," Charlotte whispered to her teammates. "Someone's coming down the stairs."

They all froze... They could hear the voices and footsteps of at least two or three crew starting down the stairwell.

(Oh no! They had no way, or place, to hide!)

HI DETECTIVE!
ANY IDEAS?? THEY CAN'T GO UP THE STAIRS, AND THEY CAN'T RUN BACK TO THE ROOM THEY JUST LEFT... HOW CAN DAX, CHARLOTTE, AND VIVIAN AVOID BEING CAUGHT?

Dax looked like he was going to bolt back toward the room they'd been hiding in, but Vivian grabbed his arm before he had a chance to move.

"You two, start kissing," she ordered Dax and Charlotte.

"Kissing??" Dax asked, completely confused. "But—"

"Just do it," she said, pushing the two together. "And make it look real."

Vivian then closed her eyes and began to change form.

By the time the three men descending the steps made it to the bottom, Vivian had completed her shapeshift: she now looked exactly like Dr. Loft (who the crew believed was Mr. Bastilia, the pupils' instructor.)

With her back to the stairwell (and Charlotte and Dax passionately kissing a few feet down the hallway), *Vivian* then started to yell at the teens.

"You two!" *Vivian* scolded her pupils. "You know the rules while aboard. We are restricted to the kitchen and our sleeping quarters only. ... What are you thinking!?"

(Charlotte immediately picked up on what Vivian was doing.).

She stopped kissing Dax, and turned to face *Vivian.*

"Leave us alone," she said rudely. "We just wanted some privacy."

Vivian then went and grabbed their wrists. "You are the most inconsiderate and selfish students I've ever taught!" *she* said in a fed-up tone. "Come with me, we're returning to the kitchen this second."

Since the three crew members who had just come down the stairs witnessed this entire exchange, they had no reason to suspect it wasn't authentic.

"Would you like some help escorting them back to the kitchen?" one of them said to *Vivian.*

"Thank you for the kind offer," *Vivian* replied. "But I'll manage fine on my own. ... I apologize for this. I should've kept a closer eye on them."

"No need to worry," the man said back, smiling about the two lovebirds who had disobeyed their teacher. "We were all teenagers once."

The other two crew members giggled and nodded, obviously remembering similar experiences from their own teenage years.

"Once again, I'm extremely sorry," *Vivian* said while leading Dax and Charlotte toward the stairwell. "I promise you my pupils will be on their best behavior from now on."

CHAPTER 24

When Dax, Charlotte, and Vivian returned to the kitchen a few minutes later, they saw the other Elite 7 members consoling Dr. Loft—who was sitting in a chair, trembling. (Dr. Loft had just spoken to Rudd Major and been told about the wholphins' brain matter being sucked out.) The poor man, who had dedicated his life to monitoring and protecting these beautiful creatures, was on the verge of a nervous breakdown.

After Zora brought them up to speed on the details Rudd Major and Vlad had just explained over the communicator, Vivian then shared what they had witnessed deep down in the ferry.

"They're currently trapping a mother and her calf?" Dr. Loft said after hearing this. "And a spaceship is coming to transport them somewhere?" (The kitchen was in the center of the ferry, and was windowless, so Dr. Loft had no idea anything like this had been happening.)

"Now we know why they wanted us in here," Screed commented. "To keep us from seeing anything."

"I refuse to let this happen," Dr. Loft said in a rage while standing up and heading for the door. "I'll cut the net myself if I have to."

"Dax, block the door," Screed quickly said while preparing to talk the irate doctor down. "Dr. Loft, I understand how frustrated you are, but we need to let this play out."

"Play out!?" the doctor yelled. "We are here, and we can do

something! Don't you kids have a conscience!?"

The doctor then began trying to physically force himself past Dax.

"Dr. Loft, please," Vivian, now standing next to Dax, pleaded. "We have to play our cards right. Attempting to stop the kidnapping would serve no beneficial purpose at all."

But the doctor, unfortunately, wouldn't listen to reason.

Although the Elite 7 didn't have an official leader, Screed knew he needed to do something before the respected doctor did something *stupid...* (Despite not wanting to use this technique on an ally, Screed decided he had no other choice.)

He closed his eyes and focused. ... He was going to use his powers to *safely subdue* the doctor.

Inflicting a headache would have been cruel, so Screed opted to just make Dr. Loft have a dizzy spell. (And since Dax was right there, there was no concern about the doctor falling and hurting himself.)

...

"Whoa—" Dr. Loft suddenly said, looking wobbly. "I think I'm hyperventilating."

While Dax held the doctor from losing his balance, Charlotte brought over a chair for him to sit on.

Screed then stopped using his powers, since the doctor now appeared a little more level-headed. (And thankfully, Dr. Loft had no clue the dizziness had been caused by Screed's mind reading powers.)

"Dr. Loft," Vivian said, squatting down so she could speak to him face to face. "As we promised when we arrived on Asos, we will figure out a way to stop what's happening. ... But we need to bust their entire operation, not just this one kidnapping."

...

"I'm sorry," the doctor said after thinking things through a bit. "And thank you for preventing me from leaving this kitchen: it would have undone all your efforts up till now."

Screed used his communicator to contact Vlad and Rudd Major. He gave them the details of the current mother-calf wholphin kidnapping that was underway, and explained that a transport ship was on its way to pick up the wholphins and then take them *somewhere.*

"Screed," Vlad said to his best friend over the communicator. "We need to follow the transport vessel after it picks up the wholphins."

"I agree," Screed replied.

"But," Rudd Major added. "We can't leave you guys down there while we follow the transport vessel. That would be far too risky…"

"There's no way to get us off the ferry that quickly," Screed said back. "Don't worry, we'll be fine."

"Unacceptable," Rudd Major said back. "And completely against mission protocol. We aren't leaving the area without you, end of discussion."

"But then you'd miss the chance to track the transport ship," Screed explained. "And we'd be back to square one."

...

"Everyone," President Artez—who was standing close to Rudd Major—then said unexpectedly. "I think I have a solution."

CHAPTER 25

"Are you out of your mind?" Captain Mazden said after listening to the president's proposal. "Those are crooks down there, lawless mercenaries-for-hire. You have no idea what they might do to you."

"I appreciate your concern," President Artez said to the worried captain. "But it's a gamble I'm willing to take."

...

The most crucial thing for President Artez's plan to succeed was *timing:* they couldn't do any of the steps too soon (or too late...)

First, Rudd Major needed to keep his ship—still cloaked, of course—a reasonable distance away, and allow the transport ship to hoist the two wholphins out of the water. They then needed to watch that ship ascend until it was out of sight.

* * *

"Alright," Rudd Major said. "The transport ship has picked up the wholphins and is almost out of Asos' atmosphere. We've got about twenty minutes to work with; any longer than that, and I'll lose the ability to track and follow it."

"Then let's do this," President Artez announced.

Rudd Major switched off the cloak and made a beeline for the ferry. (The ferry crew would spot them soon, so they needed to announce their arrival before being asked any questions.)

Rudd Major nodded to the president, indicating he had opened a communication channel with the ferry.

"This is President Artez," she said in a powerful (but calm) tone. "We are here to take the pupils and their teacher back to land."

(Then they waited to see what the reply would be…)

"President Artez?" the captain of the ferry said back. "How… unexpected. … We were planning on sailing to land shortly, so there's really no need to—"

"A pupil's doctor called me," the president said back. "He said his young patient, the one suffering from brutal headaches, needs to be brought to his clinic immediately. When it comes to the safety of our youth, I'm not taking any risks."

* * *

The evil captain looked to his crew for advice. They couldn't say *"No"* to Asos' leader, as that would draw immediate unwanted attention. (In addition, that act could even put them at risk of being arrested.)

"Understood," the captain then said back. "We'll have them waiting for you up top. I assume your vessel has cables?"

"Yes, it does," the president responded. "We'll position our ship above your ferry shortly."

…

Now hovering in the correct position, Rudd Major pushed the button to open the hatch on the bottom of his vessel.

The president saluted, double-checked she was hooked up to the cable safely, and gave the thumbs-up that he was ready to be lowered.

…

"President Artez," the captain said while shaking Asos' leader's hand. "You didn't need to come down here yourself. We could've helped secure the cables before hoisting each person up."

"Perhaps I'm too much of a worry wart," the president lied. "I guess it's because they're kids."

Since there were two cables, they'd be going up in twos. The president helped Screed (who was still pretending to be in pain) get hooked up to one cable, and the evil captain helped Vivian get secured into the other.

...

Once those two were both aboard Rudd Major's ship, the cables came back down, and Florence and Zora went next. And right after that, they moved onto lifting Charlotte and Dax.

While Charlotte and Dax were on their way up, President Artez made sure to keep the conversation light and friendly. "We're so grateful you rescued and watched over this group," she praised the captain. "Their families are going to be so relieved."

"Any captain would have done the same," the captain said back. "I'm just glad we happened to be in the area to help. I don't want to think of what would've happened if they'd been left to float at sea for days."

...

And finally, Dr. Loft (still posing as the teacher, of course) and the president hooked themselves into the two cables.

After thanking the captain again and wishing them the best, they signaled to the ship to begin hoisting them up.

...

Dr. Loft was being lifted, but President Artez's cable hadn't even become taut yet. She looked up, wondering what the delay was.

Dax stuck his head out and yelled, "There's something wrong with your cable! The reel isn't working!"

President Artez rolled her eyes. "Well, we can't wait forever for it to be fixed!" she yelled back. "Once you get Mr. Bastilia aboard, lower his cable back down for me."

The president then turned to face the captain. "This is why regular safety checks are mandatory on Asos," she commented. "The owner of that vessel is in for a big fine, even though he's helping us today."

...

With the unusable cable now dangling, the functioning one was being lowered for the president.

"As soon as we get the kids back home," she told the captain, "we'll let you know."

"Safe journeys, President Artez," the captain smiled.

But after signaling for them to hoist her up, nothing happened...

"You've got to be kidding me," the president groaned, looking at the captain in embarrassment.

"President Artez!" Dax shouted down. "This one isn't working either, now! We think it's a problem with the battery, but—"

The president, now angry, undid the cable from her belt. She then looked up and shouted, "That pupil needs to be taken to his doctor immediately! Manually pull up the cables, close the hatch, and race him to land!"

"But—" Dax went to say back.

"That was an order!" the president yelled even louder.

"Yes, ma'am," Dax said back, doing exactly as instructed.

"I apologize about this," the president said as the teens aboard Rudd Major's ship began pulling the dangling cables up hand over hand. "If you direct me to your helm, I'll contact another ship to come and get me, although they might not be able to do so until tomorrow morning."

(The president's ruse had worked! The Elite 7 were all back with Rudd Major—in time to now tail the transport ship. Plus, the ferry crew certainly wouldn't harm or kidnap any more wholphins while the president was on board!)

CHAPTER 26

Rudd Major breathed a sigh of relief to finally have the entire Elite 7 team back on his vessel. (But since this had only been possible because of the risk President Artez was taking, he kept his emotions contained.)

"Will we be able to catch up to that ship?" Screed asked as they were leaving the atmosphere. "Or are they going too fast?"

"You underestimate the power of this old, trusty spaceship," Rudd Major replied, grinning. "It may not look like much, but when given enough juice, can fly like the wind."

"Any idea where we're heading?" Captain Mazden then inquired.

"I've tried extrapolating their current flight path," Rudd Major replied. "But there are too many star systems that could be their potential destination."

...

"Once we do arrive wherever they're going," Florence said a few minutes later. "What's our game plan?"

Although that was a fairly straightforward question, the answer to it was something no one could easily provide...

"My primary concern," Dr. Loft commented, "is protecting the wholphins. And by that, I mean both rescuing the ones being experimented on, and also putting a stop to further killings and kidnappings."

"I'd say the first thing we need to do," Florence suggested, "is spy on exactly what they're doing. We need to know what, and who, we're up against."

"I like that plan," Dax agreed. "Gather as much intel as we can, and then we'll be better prepared to take down the whole operation when the time is right."

"And for now," Rudd Major then said, "and I know I have no authority here—I want all seven of you to go grab some shuteye. You're all sleep-deprived to some degree, and now might be the only time to lie down for a nap."

"Yes, boss," Dax laughed, heading toward the room that had foldout cots in it. "Although I don't know how well the others will sleep once I start sawing logs."

"Maybe another kiss from Charlotte would put a stop to your snoring?" Vivian commented, grinning.

"*Another* kiss?" Zora reacted, watching Charlotte's face turn red. "I didn't know there had been a first one."

"It happened right in front of me," Vivian told everyone.

"You young folks," Rudd Major laughed. "I just can't seem to keep up on who's dating who."

"Well, back when you were young," Captain Mazden commented to Rudd Major, "you dated countless girls. ... Don't tell me you've forgotten about those days??"

(Now Rudd Major was the one with the red face!)

* * *

A few hours later (while the teens had been catching some z's), they had managed to catch up to the transport ship. (Rudd Major kept his ship cloaked and back by a few kilometers, just to be safe.)

"Mornin'," Rudd Major remarked as Screed came out from the room he'd been sleeping in. "Nice nap?"

"I think so," he replied. "It feels like we've slowed down. Have we finally caught up to them?"

"Yup," Rudd Major said, pointing to the vessel flying ahead of them. "Why don't you get some more sleep; I'll let you know when they start approaching a planet."

"Nah, I'll just hang out here," Screed answered. "Dax's snoring is way too loud."

Vlad then came out as well.

"You, too?" Screed asked his friend.

"How does Dax not wake himself up?" Vlad commented, laughing a bit. "That's gotta be the loudest snoring I've ever heard."

* * *

After a couple more hours of flying (and with everyone awake and back on the bridge again), Rudd Major noticed the vessel they were tailing had just changed its speed (and slightly altered its trajectory.)

"We must be getting close," Rudd Major told everyone. "Let me put up a map of this region, and see exactly where we're headed."

Rudd Major then gulped...

And his face went white.

"What's wrong?" Vlad—who had yet to look up at the map—asked.

Screed tapped his friend's shoulder and pointed at the system of stars displayed on the screen.

"The transport ship is on course for Vos," Screed said, barely believing it himself.

"Vos!?" Vlad reacted. "But that's... impossible. Vos is cloaked: There's no way a ship could head to Vos; They don't even know it exists."

"I'm equally shocked," Rudd Major admitted. "But like it or

not, they have been provided with our home planet's exact location…"

…

Everyone's shock amplified while following the transport ship into Vos' atmosphere: The ship they were tailing appeared to be heading to The Interstellar Detective Academy!

…

The ship didn't set down at the school itself, but instead at an area a few kilometers north of it.

"I'm speechless," Rudd Major told everyone, getting his ship's camera to zoom in on what was happening down below. "It looks like there is a big, camouflaged door on the side of that mountain: That must be where they have some sort of conduit or pipe to get the wholphins inside."

"And I bet that's the only way in or out of the mountain," Vlad then said. "If we want to sneak inside to spy, now might be our only chance."

"I'll set us down as close as I can without kicking up too must dust, as that that would give our presence away," Rudd Major said while searching for a suitable place to land. "You guys quickly sort out who's going inside."

CHAPTER 27

Since there was no time to discuss who would be the most suitable to go, Screed quickly made that decision for everyone. He split up the Elite 7 into two teams: the group that would go inside to spy, and the group that would *"rescue the spy team if necessary."*

Screed had selected himself, Vlad, Florence, and Vivian as the spy group. (And since everyone trusted his judgment, no one questioned his selections or complained.)

"Flo, bolt to the entrance and scope things out," Screed told her once Rudd Major had landed and lowered the ramp. "Find a rock or tree or something to hide behind, and we'll get there as fast as we can."

Florence's leg speed allowed her to zoom to where she was headed in no time at all. She then ducked behind a pile of bushes about 20 or 30 meters to the right of the open doors.

She watched as a large tube-like slide—which reminded her of the ones at the waterslide park she'd been to a few times—mechanically extended from inside the mountain (until it connected with the tank in the transport ship.) Once staff had confirmed it was connected and properly sealed, they flipped a switch to start the movement of the wholphins.

The engineers of this contraption knew what they were doing: The spot where the tube connected to the transport ship's tank was slightly above where it attached to a tank inside the facility, meaning gravity would take the water (and wholphins) down the slide effortlessly.

...

By the time Screed, Vad, and Vivian got to where Florence was, the wholphins were now inside the secret facility, and the tube had been disconnected from the tank (and was currently being retracted).

"Guys, we don't have much time," Screed—still breathing heavily from the dash over—said quietly to his team. "They'll probably be closing the entrance soon."

Vlad started going invisible. "I'll rush in now," he said, "and I'll report everything I see via communicator."

"No," Screed said back right away. "We're not letting you go in alone."

"Alright," Vlad—now completely invisible—commented. "I'll go in now, make sure the coast is clear for you guys to come in before the doors shut, and then I'll signal you."

"But we can't see you," Vivian pointed out. "How are you going to—"

"Plus, we don't want to use our communicators unless absolutely necessary," Screed added. "Just in case they have technology here scanning for that type of thing."

"Gotcha," Vlad replied. "I'll find a way to signal you: just keep your eyes peeled on the entrance."

...

When Vlad walked through the big entrance doors, he realized right away that he was standing on a raised, steel platform (similar to the scaffolding erected around buildings when repairs or painting is being done.)

On both ends of this long, narrow platform were stairs, which led to the platform below. (And if one were to keep going down from platform to platform, they'd eventually make it to the ground, which was at least 7 or 8 meters below where Vlad was standing.

The *mesmerizing thing* was what had been constructed in front of this scaffolding; There was an enormous tank, much bigger than anything he'd ever seen at an aquarium. Vlad ballparked the width as about 10 meters, slightly bigger than the height.

As much as he wanted to focus on what was inside the tank, Vlad knew the top priority was getting his teammates in here unnoticed. (And since the noise of staff descending the stairs had just stopped, Vlad guessed someone would soon be pushing the button to close the doors.)

Vlad then spotted a switch next to the entrance. His eyes followed the wires that went out from that switch... up to the overhead lights! (Could this be an amazingly simple solution??)

Vlad flicked the switch, and all the lights went off, plunging everything in here into darkness.

"What the—!?" he heard one of the men down below yell. "Must be a problem with the generators. Someone go check that out, quickly."

* * *

"Now that's what I call a *not-so-subtle* signal," Screed laughed, shaking his head. "I guess the next best thing to being invisible is being in the dark. No one will see us, eh?"

Screed, Florence, and Vivian sprinted to the entrance, where they knew Vlad must be waiting for them.

"Stop as soon as you walk in. Stop as soon as you walk in," Vlad said in a voice just above a whisper. (He needed to be quiet enough to make sure no one down below would hear him.)

...

"Squat down," Vlad then said. "The platform is solid, so they'll never see you up here unless you stick your face out over the edge."

Since they needed the lights back on to see what was happening, Vlad went back to the switch. He flipped it on and off a few times (to hopefully fool the people working here into thinking it had been an electricity issue), and then finally he left it in the up position.

They could hear voices down below them, and although they couldn't make out the specifics of the conversations, they guessed there were at least three or four people.

The stairs leading down from one platform to the next always descended into the middle of the lower platform. Screed and his friends could therefore move down a couple of levels without being seen (as long as they did so very quietly.)

...

After tiptoeing down two platforms, they kneeled down and looked out at the massive tank in front of them. What was inside was a combination of *breathtaking* and *disturbing,* though...)

There were at least 12 or 13 wholphins inside (only one of which was big enough to be an adult: likely the one that had just arrived today.)

But... the wholphins weren't alone in the tank; There were also two scientists (in full scuba gear), who were at the bottom of the tank, watching a baby wholphin that was in some sort of cage.

"The only adult wholphin keeps circling that cage," Screed whispered. "That must be her baby they are about to experiment on."

One of the scientists uncapped a hypodermic needle. He then put his arm in the cage, stabbed the baby wholphin with that needle, and injected something into its blubber.

He then signaled thumbs-up to his partner, who opened up the gate to the cage, allowing the panicking baby to reunite with its mother.

...

The spying teens then heard two sets of footsteps down below (which were gradually getting louder), and walking at what sounded like a fast pace.

"We would like an update," a woman's voice said right after the walking noise stopped.

"The newest brain-growth serum has been injected into wholphin 27," one of the scientists answered. "The one that just arrived today. Every 24 hours, we'll draw some blood to see if the markers we are hoping will increase actually rise or not."

Screed lightly nudged Vlad and whispered, "Go invisible again, and poke your head over the ledge."

Vlad nodded, and got ready to peer down at what was happening about 4 meters below.

"Screed," Florence said softly. "If two people just arrived, there must be another way to get in here."

"True," Screed agreed. "We'll need to look into that as soon as it's safe to do so."

Since Screed, Florence, and Vivian couldn't see Vlad, they had no idea if he had completed his visual inspection yet or not. But... they heard his breathing suddenly speed up, as if something was troubling him.

"You okay?" Vivian asked him quietly.

Vlad was so overwhelmed that he couldn't keep himself invisible. (Luckily, his friends had noticed him reverting back, and they quickly pulled him away from the ledge before anyone spotted him.)

"Vlad, what's going on?" Screed asked Vlad (whose face was now white.)

"It's..." Vlad said, trembling. "Ms. ... Ms. Flaxton. ... And Mr. Lexington."

"Ms. Flaxton??" Florence reacted. "The head of The Interstellar Detective Agency? What would—"

"And Mr. Lexington?" Screed also commented. "We know he

had to stop teaching here because he was secretly injecting himself with something in that hidden mind reading experimentation room we discovered before. ... This makes zero sense, though. What's going on??"

CHAPTER 28

This unfathomable development was too much for Screed and his team to process; What had started as a *simple mission to Asos* had somehow led them all the way back to their school—to then learn that the head of The Agency was behind the wholphin killings and kidnappings. This went completely against what The Agency stood for... (There was no way The Agency's Board of Directors would have approved such a brutal and unforgiving act. Nothing made sense...)

They then heard Ms. Flaxton speak again. "We are pleased with the progress," she said. "Thanks to your dedication, we are getting closer and closer to our goal."

(Our goal??)

"Anyway," she went on. "My assistant and I are heading back to review all the new data. Plus, I need to check if any more wholphins have been spotted. ... Please join us in the special lab when you finish up here."

Since Screed, Florence, and Vlad still appeared to be in a state of disbelief, Vivian was the one who reacted.

"Guys, we've gotta get Vlad to follow Ms. Flaxton and Mr. Lexington," she commented. "If he goes invisible, he can easily tail them."

"I'm not sure he's up for that right now," Screed said, pointing to how panicked Vlad still looked. "Let's just—"

"Wait, I can do this," Vlad then said, starting to go invisible. "If I don't, then we'll have no way of finding out who else is part of this crime ring."

Florence took Vlad's hands just before he disappeared. "Vlad, you don't have to go," she said, worried. "We can figure out another way. We—"

(But her next words were cut off by a pair of invisible lips being pressed up against hers!)

"I got this," he said after kissing her for a few seconds. "You guys sneak back out, tell Rudd Major what's going on, and I'll update you as soon as I can."

Then Vlad, being as quiet as possible, quickly made his way down—so he'd get to the bottom in time to follow Ms. Flaxton and Mr. Lexington.

One of the men below then made an announcement to the scientists in the tank. "You guys should surface and climb out," he told them. "The boss and her assistant will probably want your help analyzing the data."

Screed and his friends began to panic. (If the divers began floating up, they'd be spotted!)

"We've still got two more wholphin blood draws to complete," one of the underwater scientists replied through a communicator installed in his scuba gear. "It shouldn't take more than a few minutes, though. After that, we'll surface."

Screed, Florene, and Vivian immediately began heading up the stairs, knowing that every second counted. (But they still needed to go slowly, as one noisy misstep would give away their presence.)

...

When they got to the entrance, they examined the closed door: It was a large, single door that slid horizontally on a rail.

Screed went to slide it open, but it wouldn't budge... There was no lock, but maybe the motor that mechanically opened and closed it was preventing them from sliding the door.

Florence and Vivian tried to help, but it was useless...

"I'll call Dax for help," Florence then said, pushing the button on her communicator.

Dax acknowledged her request, and he, Charlotte, and Zora began sprinting to the entrance.

...

"Blood draws are done," they heard one of the underwater scientists announce. "Once we double-check we haven't left any blood vials behind, we'll surface."

"Understood," one of the men down below replied.

...

"Vials are packed up," a scientist inside the tank said a couple of minutes later. "Surfacing now."

"Roger that," a voice replied. "See you shortly."

There was no way to tell how close Dax was, but there was nothing they could do now other than wait. (Screed knew scuba divers surfaced slowly, so they likely still had a few minutes to work with.)

"Should we kill the lights?" Florence then suggested. "That might buy us a bit more time."

"It would," Vivian mentioned. "But then they'd see light shoot in from outside when Dax forces the door open."

"Tell you what," Screed said. "If the divers are getting close to where they'd see us, then we'll turn off the lights. Let's give Dax a bit more time, first."

Vivian peered over the platform's ledge. "They're about

halfway up the tank," she told Screed and Florence. "Another minute or so, and they'll be lookin' right at us."

...

Creak!

(Dax had just yanked the sliding door open about 50 or 60 centimeters: He was holding it open just enough for them to slip through!)

"Hurry," Screed said, motioning for Florence and Vivian to go out first.

And right after that, Screed exited (and Dax let the door reclose.)

"Where's Vlad?" Charlotte asked. "Or is he invisible and I just can't see him?"
"Vlad's following Ms. Flaxton and Mr. Lexington," Screed answered. "Now c'mon, we need—"
"Flaxton and Lexington!?" Charlotte said in shock. "What—"
"I'll explain when we get back to the ship," Screed replied while starting to run. "We have to get Rudd Major to fly us to The Academy's front door."
"We can't go into our school," Vivian said. "We're supposed to be training on—"
"I know," Screed told her, understanding they didn't have a plan yet. "But we'll figure something out... at least I hope we can."

CHAPTER 29

The color drained out of Rudd Major's face immediately after Screed told him that the head of The Agency was behind all this... (Rudd Major had dedicated well over half of his life to upholding The Agency's goals and protocols. What he had just learned was unimaginable...)

"Are you absolutely positive it was her?" Rudd Major asked the team.

"Well, Vlad was the only one who got a look at her," Screed replied. "But I can't imagine he'd make a mistake."

"And did anyone refer to her," Rudd Major asked next, "or Mr. Lexington, by name?"

"The scientists called her *'The boss,'*" Florence answered. "And she referred to Mr. Lexington as *'her assistant.'*"

"So, there is a possibility that Vlad was wrong," Rudd Major commented.

"Very unlikely," Charlotte mentioned. "I'd say the more likely thing is that the scientists were contracted privately, and have no idea of the names or positions of who they are working for."

"The complexity of their whole operation," Rudd Major sighed, "and the efforts they are putting in to keep it secretive, scare me to the core... How do we know who to trust anymore? How can we even—"

"Grampa," Vivian said, hugging Rudd Major from behind. "I know this is pretty overwhelming, but we have to maintain our focus and ignore feelings of betrayal or rage."

"Thank you," he smiled, appreciative that such a young person could have such mature thinking. Then he turned to Screed. "What's our course of action?" he asked.

"We'll need to sneak into the school at some point soon," Screed replied. "But not until we hear from Vlad; We have to wait to find out where we need to go."

"But how can we move through the school unnoticed?" Zora asked.

"I'm still working on that," Screed replied (honestly) while shrugging his shoulders.

5 tense minutes passed.

And 5 more.

(Everyone was on pins and needles, but knew they needed to sit tight and wait.)

...

Bleep.

"Incoming message from Vlad," Rudd Major said, putting it up on the main screen so no one would have to look down at their small handheld communicators.

> *I need two teams in here: One should go to the mind reading experimentation room. The other needs to meet me in the school's old wing. I'll be waiting on the stairs, halfway between the first and second floor. And Charlotte must be part of the team that comes to meet me.*

Screed quickly instructed Rudd Major to send a short reply.

Understood. We'll be there as soon as possible.

Screed then turned around and told his teammates to double-check that their backpacks weren't missing anything.

"Zora, Dax," Screed said, quickly deciding who would go where. "You're with Charlotte: you guys go meet Vlad. Flo, Viv, you come with me to the mind reading experimentation room."

"Detectives," Rudd Major said before opening the ramp. "Please be careful. Your school probably doesn't feel intimidating, but trust me, this is by far your most dangerous mission to date."

"We'll keep you posted on our progress," Screed told his trusted liaison.

The six detectives then exited Rudd Major's cloaked vessel and began making their way to the school's front door (hiding behind trees and bushes along the way.)

...

They were now crouching down near the big flowerbed and memorial statue that was off to the right of the front doors. The final part of the dash inside would only take about 30 seconds, but once they entered, they had no idea if the hallways would be bare.

Zora looked at her watch. "Well, period three began a few minutes ago," she said quietly. "All students will be in classrooms."

"And since it's pretty cold today," Dax added. "The classroom doors will be closed to keep the chilly hallway air out."

"But..." Screed worried. "Not every teacher has a period three lecture; What if one of them happens to be roaming the hallway when—"

"Teachers hate the cold hallways as much as students do," Dax pointed out. "Any instructor with a period off will be in the teachers' lounge sipping hot coffee."

...

"Then let's do this," Screed nodded, preparing to lead his team into the school.

...

But just before he stood up to lead the dash, Screed heard a voice! (But he wasn't hearing it with his ears, it was inside his head...)

Wait where you are.
It's not safe right now.

Screed then spun around and held his arms out, ensuring that everyone stayed put.
"Why aren't we going?" Dax asked, confused. "C'mon, the coast is clear: It's now or never."
"Hold on," Screed said, motioning for everyone to squat down again.

...

Hiding again, they peered over at the entrance.

The door opened... and out walked Mr. Gatwick!

"It's Mr. Gatwick, the school janitor," Charlotte whispered. "Think he spotted us from a window or something?"
Screed then realized what was going on! (The voice he'd heard in his head was coming from Mr. Gatwick, who Screed knew was a mind reader capable of communicating through thoughts.)
Since no one other than Screed knew of that special power (and because of the fact Mr. Gatwick had told Screed to keep it secret from others), he decided he should honor that request.

"Mr. Gatwick is on our side," Screed told his friends. "Trust me, he'll help us; He confided in Vlad and I before."

Mr. Gatwick seemed to know where the detectives were hiding; He walked straight over to their location behind the statue and bushes.

"I just happened to spot you while wiping the upstairs windows," the janitor lied while winking at Screed. "I know why you're here. ... And I know I can help."

"You can help us?" Zora asked, confused.

"You need to get somewhere without being spotted, I assume," Mr. Gatwick said. "I can lead the way. ... I wander the halls all day, right? I'll make sure the coast is clear at each corner before giving you the okay to follow me. As long as we continue like that, you'll never get spotted."

"Brilliant," Florence nodded.

"Hold on," Screed said next. "We are splitting into two teams once inside: You can only guide one of the groups."

"I beg to differ," Mr. Gatwick smiled, looking at Vivian.

...

"You should've been a detective," Screed grinned once he realized what the janitor was suggesting.

Vivian, after studying the janitor's appearance a little more closely, began shapeshifting to look just like him.

...

"Take this rag and mop with you," Mr. Gatwick said while passing them to her. "As you all know, I carry those two things pretty much everywhere."

Since Screed, Florence, and Vivian (who was now the spitting image of Mr. Gatwick) had further to go, they went into the school first.

(The second group would wait a few minutes, and then enter the school to make their way to where Vlad would meet up with them.)

CHAPTER 30

Vivian (now the spitting image of Mr. Gatwick) opened the front door to the school and peered inside. ... As hoped and expected, there wasn't a single person in the chilly hallway.

She put one hand behind her back and gave Screed and Florence a thumbs-up: indicating it was safe for them to follow her in.

They cautiously made their way through the school's halls: only proceeding down each new corridor after *Vivian* had confirmed it was empty.

...

When they arrived at the old wing and went into the janitor's closet (where the hidden path to the mind reading experimentation room began), they finally breathed a sigh of relief.

Before pulling the hammer (which was really a *switch* to open the hidden path), Screed entered an update into his communicator that would go to the other team and the ship.

> *Now in the janitor's closet. Will proceed to the mind reading experimentation room.*

There was no need for Vivian to continue the shapeshift any longer, so she reverted to her usual self. Screed then pulled up on the hammer, and the secret entrance opened.

...

When they got close to the mind reading experimentation room, they noticed all the lights in the room were on. They got down on their hands and knees, to make sure they wouldn't be seen through the windows if someone was in there.

"And remember," Screed quietly reminded his team, "don't go past that yellow line. If you do, it triggers an alarm."

Vivian and Florence both nodded in understanding.

"Screed," Florence whispered to him softly. "It doesn't look like anyone's in there... but I think I hear something."

Vivian stretched her head up just far enough to get a clear view through the window. (And by the shocked expression on her face, she'd seen something she wasn't expecting!)

"Mr. Lexington is lying on the floor in there, squirming a bit and mumbling to himself," she told Screed and Florence. "And on the table next to him, there's a used syringe."

"That means he's just tested a vial on himself," Screed told her.

"Tested to do what?" Vivian asked.

"I can't say for sure," Screed replied. "But my best guess is that he's trying to permanently enhance his mind reading powers."

The three detectives stayed crouched down and listened to the garbled-up gibberish coming from Mr. Lexington. (This was likely happening because the chemical he'd injected himself with was overwhelming his system.)

"Viv," Screed said while passing her a pair of binoculars. "Stick your head up again, and use these to read what's displaying on the computer screen in there. I'll stand up a bit, too: and make sure Mr. Lexington isn't looking in our direction.

...

"It's showing a list of tested vials," Vivian said. "With notes on each one's effectiveness. And his name is at the top of the screen, so these must be ones he's used on himself."

They both squatted down again.

"I need you to check one more thing," Screed then told Vivian. "Look for which ones are displaying the highest effectivity percentages, and tell me the vial numbers for those."

"Gotcha," she nodded, getting ready to use the binoculars again.

...

"The ones with the highest effectivity numbers," Vivian told Screed, "all start with VF-11."

"Hold on, I gotta write that down," Screed said.

"And it looks like the one he's testing now, "Vivian went on, "which currently has a blank in the results column, is VF-12 vial 1."

"Then the VF-12 batch must be the newest," Screed commented.

"Let me try to focus on the cabinet for sec to see what's in there," she started to say after adjusting her position a bit. ... "It's empty, actually. ... Maybe they no longer store the—"

Beep! Beep! Beep!

Florence pointed at Vivian's right foot, which was sticking out past the yellow line.

"Oh, no," Vivian panicked, ducking back down. "I accidentally set the alarm off."

"Who's out there!?" Mr. Lexington yelled from the floor inside the room. "I told you I'd report this sample's result when I was finished! Be patient!"

HI DETECTIVE!
THESE THREE ARE SURE IN A PICKLE, AREN'T THEY?? ANY IDEAS ABOUT HOW THEY CAN REPLY TO MR. LEXINGTON'S QUESTION WITHOUT DRAWING ANY SUSPICION?

CHAPTER 31

Completely unaware of the predicament Screed, Florence, and Vivian were currently in, the team of Zora, Dax, and Charlotte—led by the *real* Mr. Gatwick—were slithering through the school's halls.

...

They only had one close call while sneaking through the corridors: A Year 4 student suddenly exited a classroom to dash to the washroom. (Luckily, Mr. Gatwick hadn't given Zora, Dax, and Charlotte the signal to round that corner yet, so the girl on her way to the washroom only saw the janitor—and him being in the halls was nothing out of the ordinary.)

...

Right after entering the school's old wing, Mr. Gatwick took the teens to the staircase, hoping Vlad was waiting there as planned.

"Dudes, you made it," a voice—from the invisible Vlad, of course—said when the janitor arrived with the three detectives. Vlad then turned off his powers so everyone could see him. "Mr. Gatwick, thanks for helping out. We owe you one."

"I just hope there's a way you can put a stop to what's going on," the janitor commented, "without putting yourself in harm's way."

"We'll be careful," Vlad commented, smiling.

"Best of luck," Mr. Gatwick nodded. "Alright, I had better get going: It'd be tough to explain my presence here in the old wing."

"Thanks again," Vlad said, giving the janitor a high-five.

...

"I hope we've still got enough time," Vlad then said to his team. "I know Ms. Flaxton is in one of the classrooms here, but I don't know which one."

"I thought you were tailing her," Zora commented. "What happened?"

"I was following her and Mr. Lexington," Vlad explained, "through a tunnel that went from the wholphins directly to the mind reading experimentation room. When we got there, Mr. Lexington got ready to inject himself, and Ms. Flaxton disappeared down the path that leads to the janitor's closet in the old wing here. I waited a little too long before starting down that path—and it was pitch-black, and I was a ways behind her—so I had to move slowly. ... Anyway, once I arrived, I tiptoed through the halls and put my ears up to all the classroom doors, but I couldn't hear anything."

"Are you sure she hasn't already left this wing?" Dax asked.

"Impossible," Vlad replied. "I have a view of the front hall from where I've been hiding in the stairwell. She hasn't left, so she's gotta be in a classroom, I'm positive."

"Then let's get to work," Zora said to the team. "What's the plan?"

Vlad smiled at Charlotte. "You're gonna have a busy day," he commented.

...

Every classroom door in the old wing was rigged up with a

heavy-duty locking mechanism: obviously installed to ensure no one got in to see whatever was being hidden behind the doors.

"Luckily," Vlad explained. "It looks like the classroom doors themselves weren't replaced when the locks were added. And they were built way back when no one cared about air drafts. Each door has a narrow gap at the bottom…"

"Which I can easily slip under," Charlotte smiled, aware she now had her work cut out for her.

"I say we start on level two," Zora suggested. "If I were trying to hide something, I would think a first-floor room, which has windows to the courtyard that could easily be smashed to climb through, would be too risky."

…

The system they used was very simple: Charlotte turned herself paper thin, and Dax carefully "partially" slid her under each door. (He slid her head under, ensuring her face was up, so she'd be able to get a look at what was going on without reverting to her normal form.)

…

The first seven rooms they inspected weren't hiding anything. There was nothing behind those locked classroom doors other than dust-covered desks (and moldy textbooks that teachers and students must've left behind.)

Charlotte was tiring, but taking a break was not an option; They needed to keep going…

…

As soon as Dax slid her head under the eighth door (which was the final classroom on the right side), Charlotte realized numerous things here were *different:* First, there wasn't a single desk in here. Instead, two rows of shelving had been brought in, and those shelves were stacked with 1-liter containers (which they now knew contained wholphin brain matter) and countless small vials (some filled, some empty), which were obviously being used for injecting people in the mind reading experimentation room (and to experiment on baby wholphins.) And off to the side was what looked like a fancy chemistry laboratory set-up: This had to be where the brain matter was being synthesized into the chemicals that were being tested.

Charlotte could also hear a faint conversation, which was weird because no one was in here...

She then realized why: This classroom had been used for science lessons in the past, so there was a small room in the back corner (which would've held equipment and supplies before.)

"Guys, she's sliding further under," Dax said to Vlad and Zora. "There must be something worth investigating in there."

Following the instructions Vlad had outlined before, Zora got ready to read Charlotte's mind. (And Charlotte knew that the instant she felt a brain itch, she was supposed to think and rethink what she'd just seen, as that would allow Zora to learn what was behind the door.)

After Zora had successfully finished reading Charlotte's mind, Charlotte reverted to her usual form and tiptoed toward the storage room door. The closer she got, the louder the voices became—but she wouldn't be able to hear clearly unless she put her ear right up against the door.

"Ms. Flaxton," a woman's voice (who Charlotte immediately recognized as being that of Headmaster Vela) said. "I've been cooperating with The Academy's initiative to conduct these tests, but you're not revealing enough about your methods, and that's making me uneasy."

"I haven't been given permission to share those details with you, Headmaster Vela," Ms. Flaxton lied.

"No one outranks you at The Academy," Headmaster Vela said back. "How can you not have the authority to—"

"Look," Ms. Flaxton said back sharply while preparing to fib again. "I'm not happy about it, either... But, you know, The Academy has archaic rules and procedures."

"I'm not complaining about their rules," Headmaster Vela confirmed. "I'm just upset that my questions are never answered; I've inquired countless times about what the grey substance is inside the containers dropped off periodically, but have never been told. Plus, your visits to the school are never announced ahead of time: you just seem to suddenly show up."

Charlotte figured she had heard enough to know the general gist of their argument: The Academy had informed the headmaster they'd be *carrying out tests* here, but hadn't told her that innocent animals were being slaughtered and kidnapped to create the chemicals used in those tests...

Charlotte made her way back to the classroom door. She went thin again and slid through the gap into the hallway.

And the instant she was out, she reverted to her normal form and outlined what she had overheard.

CHAPTER 32

"I said who's out there!? Can't you hear me!?" Mr. Lexington yelled again from inside the mind reading experimentation room. "Anyway... Hold on, I'll unlock the door so you can come in."

(Screed, Florence, and Vivian realized that Mr. Lexington was about to stand up—but as soon as he did, they'd be busted!)

Without any time to discuss what to do, Screed did the first (and only) idea that came to him: He quickly used his powers to send a strong wave of dizziness into Mr. Lexington's mind, which would delay him from getting up for an extra 10 or 15 seconds.
"Woah..." Mr. Lexington said. "This highly concentrated injection I gave myself seems to be messing with my balance. ... I can't risk falling and hitting my head, so I'm just going to crawl over to let you in."

(They'd just bought themselves a tiny bit of time... but would that help at all??)

Vivian then thought of a way to possibly save their hides!

Instead of wasting a few valuable seconds telling Screed and Florence what she was going to do, she just started to shapeshift. She began by transforming her face and neck (which would allow her to produce the voice of the person she was shapeshifting into even before the body transformation was complete.)

Vivian was becoming Ms. Flaxton!

"Sorry for coming back here so soon," Vivian (in an excellent impression of Ms. Flaxton's voice) said loudly so Mr. Lexington could hear clearly. "I'm just eager to see if we've finally achieved the results we've been aiming for."

"I had a feeling it was you," Mr. Lexington commented. "But we'll need to give my body a bit more time to see the effects."

Vivian had completed the shapeshift, and Mr. Lexington was crawling closer to the door. (But the second he opened it, he'd see Screed and Florence, who had nowhere to hide!)

"Just let me pull myself up," Mr. Lexington then said, getting ready to stand up so he could let Vivian in.

Despite being in a state of panic, Screed knew what he and Florence needed to do. He pointed toward the exit to communicate where they were headed and then started crawling as fast as he could.

As soon as they were both safely hidden in the darkness of the tunnel, *Vivian*—who had been talking constantly to Mr. Lexington in the hopes of keeping his attention on her (and therefore not noticing Screed and Florence slithering away), was relieved her friends hadn't been caught.

...

"It's so dark in here," Florence said to Screed. "We're gonna need to use our flashlights."

"Too risky," Screed said. "If someone happens to be coming from the other end, they'd realize we're here."

"So, we have to slide along this tunnel in the dark, then?" Florence asked Screed.

"Unfortunately, yes," he replied. "I'll lead; Use one hand to grab my shirt or backpack or something. ... We'll be fine."

CHAPTER 33

"Can you guys hear something?" Vlad said softly to Charlotte, Zora, and Dax. (All four of them were back in the stairwell between floors one and two of the old wing, getting ready to brainstorm ideas about what to do next.)

"I think someone's arriving," Charlotte commented. "It sounds like a pair of voices."

"I'm gonna go invisible," Vlad then said. "I'll head downstairs to check it out."

"But what do we do if Ms. Flaxton or Headmaster Vela leave the classroom?" Zora asked. "Or if whoever just came in downstairs heads this way? We've got nowhere to hide."

"If one of those things happens, I'll create a *distraction* or something," Vlad told his team.

When Vlad (now invisible) got to the first floor, he saw who had just arrived: It was Screed and Florence!

Vlad started running toward them (but seemed to forget he was still invisible!)

...

"Vlad??" Screed asked loudly after hearing the sound of running feet. "Is that you?"

Vlad immediately turned off his powers and made an exaggerated *"Shh!"* gesture to them.

"Ms. Flaxton and Headmaster Vela are upstairs," he told

them. "We have to be quiet."

(The two groups needed some time to compare notes, but doing so in this building would be too risky...)

"Let's go to the equipment shed, you know, the one for the exercise grounds," Screed suggested. "It's pretty close to the backdoor of the old wing: We should be able to get there without being spotted."

"You guys go," Vlad replied while signaling Dax, Zora, and Charlotte to come down from the stairwell. "I'm gonna go invisible again: I'll wait near the room Ms. Flaxton and Headmaster Vela are in, and update you when they leave. ... Hey, where's Viv?"

"In the mind reading experimentation room," Screed answered. "Pretending to be Ms. Flaxton."

"But Mr. Lexington's in there too, right?" Vlad asked back. "With his enhanced mind reading powers, he'll easily figure out it's Vivian."

"Viv's pretty good at thinking on her feet," Screed reassured his best friend. "She'll be fine."

...

Now in the old (and very cold) sports equipment shed, the two teams quickly updated each other.

...

"This is very perplexing," Screed commented, unable to understand why the head of The Interstellar Detective Agency was doing what she was doing. "And why isn't Ms. Flaxton telling Headmaster Vela everything?"

...

"So, who should we report all this to?" Zora asked. "You know, who do you think would help us put a stop to what's going on?"

"As much as I hate to say this," Screed answered. "No one would listen to us if we made this information public. Ms. Flaxton has the authority to permanently oust us from the Academy, and she'd do exactly that before an inquiry even took place."

"So, what you're saying," Dax asked for confirmation, "is that we've gotta do this on our own?"

"Unfortunately, that's our only option," Screed told him.

As they tried to come up with a feasible plan, a communication came in from Vlad.

> *Both just left the classroom.*
> *I'm going to tail Ms. Flaxton.*
> *I'll update you again soon.*

"Guys," Zora said, brainstorming aloud. "I'm sorry if this analogy sounds like something out of a medieval adventure tale, but... um... it seems we currently *can't defeat the dragon*—and by that I mean Ms. Flaxton, of course. ... But, what we can do is stop it from flying and breathing fire and—"

"Beautiful analogy," Screed smiled (while the others looked completely baffled.) "I see what you're saying. We do everything we can to stall and set back their research."

"And then we'll have bought ourselves a little more time," Charlotte agreed, "to figure out exactly when and how to expose Ms. Flaxton."

"Makes sense to me," Florence nodded. "And I think I have a suggestion... Well, two suggestions, to be honest."

"Cool, let's hear," Screed said, encouraging Florence to outline her idea.

CHAPTER 34

The clever plan Florence suggested would involve tackling two tasks, but was going to actually require them splitting into three groups (one of which would have to travel a long distance!)
Screed sent a message to Rudd Major, as he needed his liaison to prep the ship for immediate launch.

> *You need to fly Zora, Dax, and me back to Asos. We are currently hiding in the sports field equipment shed. Is there any place close by where you can pick us up?*

A reply came quickly.

> *There's a patch of flat land a few hundred meters north of the sports ground. You should be able to get there easily without being seen. I'll arrive at that spot to pick you up shortly.*

Screed, Dax, and Zora then got ready to leave the shed.

"Follow me," Dax said while opening the door. "We're gonna sneak along near the right-side bleachers: That area can't be seen from the main school building."

"So, you've done lots of sneaking around, eh??" Charlotte commented, lightly punching Dax's shoulder.

"Save the sweet talk for later." Vivian laughed, recalling how happy Charlotte had been after kissing Vlad back on the ferry. "But feel free to give him a *see you soon peck* if you want."

(Although she was just being sarcastic and silly, Charlotte took Vivian's remark as *advice*. ... She grabbed Dax's arms, spun him around, and planted a huge kiss right on his lips!)

"Now you've got a good reason to make it through your mission safely," Charlotte then said to Dax. "Unless you're already, umm... seeing someone?"

Dax's face went extremely red. "Me? Seeing someone?" he said, fumbling over his words. "Definitely not. I—"

"Alright, let's go," Zora then said, pushing Dax toward the open shed door. "She likes you. You like her. Don't say something stupid to ruin it."

...

The remaining detectives now had to split into two teams to carry out a "fairly simple" task (but doing so without getting caught was going to be tricky...)

Florence sent a short message to Vlad.

> *You need to get back to the mind reading experimentation room ASAP. Make sure Mr. Lexington and the scientists don't come to the old wing.*

Vlad's reply came quickly.

> *Roger that. On my way now.*

Charlotte and Florence then went back upstairs and walked over to the door of the room that Ms. Flaxton and Headmaster Vela had previously been in.

"This will probably take me quite a while to finish," Charlotte said before getting ready to go paper-thin.

"Just take your time and do it carefully," Florence said back. "Vlad, Viv and I will do what's necessary to keep the scientists away until you're done."

CHAPTER 35

Since Vlad had been tailing Ms. Flaxton, he had quite a distance to cover to get back to the mind reading experimentation room.

...

When he arrived at that room's entrance—through the secret tunnel that was connected to the school's old wing—he saw *Ms. Flaxton* (who he knew was a shapeshifting Vivian) and Mr. Lexington inside the room.

(But the door was shut and locked! Vlad had no way to get in...)

Vlad's mind began running through possible ways to get Vivian's attention. He briefly considered knocking on the glass windows as a method to communicate his presence here to Vivian, but then decided against it—as Mr. Lexington would hear the knocking too (and then might use his enhanced mind reading powers to figure out what was going on.)

...

Vlad walked up to the window and watched as *Vivian* stood over Mr. Lexington (who was now sitting on a chair in front of the computer.) Vlad couldn't hear what they were discussing, but her body language made it clear that she was worried and scared.

(She was probably trying to say things she thought *the real Ms. Flaxton* would say, but odds were she couldn't pull off this ruse much longer...)

Vlad then saw a secret passage open: the one he remembered led to the big tank with the wholphins in it.

Four scientists walked through it, and went directly to the door of the mind reading experimentation room.

"Boss," one of them said loudly while looking through the door. "Sorry about the delay."

Vivian froze... (Should she go over and let them in?? Or would that be too risky??)

...

Before she could make up her mind, Mr. Lexington stood up, walked over to the door, and opened it up for the scientists.

"I thought you told us to meet you in the usual room, boss?" the first scientist into the room asked *Vivian*. "You know, in the room in the old wing where we synthesize the chemicals."

(Vivian had to think of a reply quickly...)

"I came to check on my assistant first," she lied. "I knew this new injection was a strong one, so I wanted to make sure he was okay."

...

Right after the fourth scientist entered, Vlad slipped in before the door closed... (He was inside!)

"Once again," another scientist said to *Vivian*. "We apologize it took us so long to finish up in the tank. One of the blood sample tubes broke while the diver was passing it out, so he had to go back down, trap the correct wholphin again, and take a new sample."

"Not to worry," *Vivian* said. "I appreciate your dedication and thoroughness."

"Come and check this out," Mr. Lexington then said, calling the scientists over to look at something on the computer screen. "We are definitely on track with the VF formulation—look how high its numbers are compared to others we've tried."

"Wow, almost off the charts," the eldest of the scientists grinned. "And those are for the previous batch, VF-11. I can't wait to see the numbers for the VF-12 vial you just tested on yourself."

"At this rate," another scientist added, "we should be able to perfect the formula within the next few weeks or months."

...

With the four scientists crowded around the computer, Vivian was now standing a few steps back.

Vlad knew that doing something like tapping Vivian's shoulder would startle her (which might cause her to yelp or scream), so he elected to whisper in her ear instead.

"Viv, it's me," Vlad said very softly into her right ear.

Vivian did jump a bit, but thankfully the scientists were too focused on the computer screen to notice.

"You and I have been assigned the task," Vlad whispered to her, "of ensuring no one goes from here to the old wing."

Vivian, of course, couldn't reply, so she just gave a tiny nod to indicate she understood.

"We need to keep them in here for at least thirty minutes, probably more," Vlad went on, speaking as softly as he could. "Do anything and everything you can to stall them."

Vivian figured the best way to keep everyone in here was to ask a question that would require a long-winded answer.

"You just said a few more weeks or months of experimenting would suffice," *Vivian* said, walking closer to the scientists. "But there's a pretty big difference between two weeks and four months. What specifically do you need to do?"

(Vivian knew the scientific answer she was about to hear would make no sense to her, but that was beside the point; She just hoped that their reply to this question would *drag on for ages.)*

CHAPTER 36

After going paper-thin and slipping under the gap at the bottom of the classroom door, Charlotte reverted to her normal form (and prepared to get started.)

She went over to the shelves containing all the test tube vial sets. Each set on the *"synthesized"* shelf contained up to 48 vials—which had been filled and were already sealed—and the sets could be easily lifted and carried by the handle in the center of each one.

Charlotte knew she was looking for the vials labeled with *VF-12* stickers—which she assumed would be on the top shelf because they were the newest ones.

"Find 'em yet?" Florence asked loudly from outside the classroom door.

...

Charlotte then spotted them. "Just located the set," she said back while carefully lifting it.

She carried it over to the counter where all the laboratory equipment was set up.

She then went back to the shelf and removed one vial from another set. She took that one to the counter and laid it down carefully.

Before beginning, Charlotte looked carefully at the VF-12 vials: The container holding them had spaces for 48 test tubes, and the only empty spot was the front-left slot (which must have held the one Mr. Lexington had recently injected into himself.)

"About to get started!" she called to Florence. "Let's hope these labels are easy to peel off..."

Charlotte wanted to do this in order, so she removed the vial in the second slot of the front row (which was to the right of the empty slot.)

She placed it on the counter, and then carefully used her fingernail to begin removing its label: which was marked *VF-12 vial 2*.

...

It took her a while to peel it off without ripping it... Luckily, it appeared that the back of the tape was still relatively sticky.

She then removed the sticker from the other vial: which had *TC-7 vial 4* written on it.

(She then looked down at the two vials, and got ready to switch the stickers.)

Finally, as planned, she taped the sticker in her left hand onto the right vial, and the one in her hand onto the left vial.

She quickly took the vial now labeled *TC-7 vial 4*—which was, of course, actually from the *VF-12* set—back to where the TC-4 set was. She placed it in carefully, making sure the label was facing forward like all the rest.

"One down, forty-six to go!" she announced to Florence. "How long did that first one take me?"

"About three and a half minutes," Florence replied. "Anyway, don't worry about trying to swap every single vial; just do as many as you can."

"Gotcha," she replied, removing a vial from the *SW-17* set to swap with the next *VF-12* vial. "Let's hope Vlad and Viv can give me another hour or so: These labels are taped on pretty well..."

* * *

For the next twenty minutes, Charlotte worked methodically. She had now managed to switch a total of six of the *VF-12* vials out, meaning about 20% of the test tubes in the *VF-12* case were actually from other sets.

"Ouch!" Charlotte suddenly yelped.

"What happened?" Florence asked back, worried.

"My finger kind of slipped while peeling the *VF-12 vial 8* label off," she replied. "The test tube fell out of my hand and smashed on the counter."

"No big deal," Florence said back. "Did you get the label off?"

"Yeah," Charlotte explained. "But some of the vial's contents got on the label and stained it.

"Tell you what," Florence advised her teammate (even though she couldn't see how bad the staining was because she was outside the classroom.) "Put that sticker on whichever random vial you'd prepared. But when putting it into the *VF-12* container, stick it somewhere in the middle where it can't be seen."

"But the vials are in order in each set," she told Florence. "The number 8 vial has gotta be in the eighth slot, which is at the far right of the first row."

"Um..." Florence mumbled, trying to come up with a solution. "Why don't you put the *vial 8* where the *18* goes, and stick the *18* in the *8's* spot? The scientists will just assume one of them made a mistake when placing them in there."

"Will do," Charlotte replied, realizing she couldn't waste too much time trying to come up with another solution. "I also need to clean up the mess from the broken vial."

Florence noticed her communicator buzz. She glanced down to see a message from Vlad.

Scientists are on their way. Get out of the classroom immediately!

CHAPTER 37

Vivian had done everything she could think of to keep the scientists in the mind reading experimentation room, but the group was overly eager to get to the classroom in the old wing to start synthesizing a new batch.

When Mr. Lexington and the scientists entered the tunnel, Vlad sent a quick message on his communicator and then began following the group.

Vivian had told Mr. Lexington and the scientists that she was *'going to check out a few more things on the computer here'* before heading to the old wing; And then the instant they were out of sight, she reverted to her normal form (as she was exhausted from holding the shapeshift for so long.)

* * *

"Charlotte, the scientists are on their way," Florence said loudly through the door.

"Yeah, I know," she replied. "I saw Vlad's message. … But I've gotta clean this gunk and broken glass."

The first thing Charlotte did was carry the *VF-12 set* back to where she had originally found it on the top shelf. She placed it in the exact same location it had been before she removed it.

"Hurry," Florence called, starting to panic. "If you don't leave that room now, we won't have enough time to run downstairs to get outside!"

"I can't leave until I clean this up," Charlotte said back. "Look, you bolt out of the building now while you still can. I'll clean this mess, go thin, and fold myself up. Tell Vlad I'll be under the file cabinet just inside the classroom door. When the scientists are walking in, all he has to do is slip his invisible hand under and pull me out..."

(Would that work??)

Florence couldn't wait another second or she'd get stuck up here (with nowhere to hide!) She used her leg speed to sprint to the stairs, down them, and then out the front door.
Breathing heavily, she hid behind some bushes and sent a message to Vlad. (She just hoped Vlad saw it in time...)
* * *
Vlad was following about 10 meters behind the scientists. (They had just exited the tunnel into the old wing a few seconds earlier, and that's when his communicator buzzed.)
As soon as he saw the message, he began jogging (throwing caution to the wind as far as being quiet was concerned.)

...

The scientists and Mr. Lexington were filing into the classroom when Vlad caught up to them. Just as the last of them walked in, Vlad did what had been explained in Florence's message.
He got on his knees and slid his left hand under the filing cabinet... and immediately felt a little "notebook" (which he knew was *Charlotte!)* Since anything Vlad held went invisible as well, the instant he grabbed the folded-up Charlotte, she vanished from view—meaning the scientists wouldn't notice a thing.

And he managed to get his arm out before the door closed!

Clasping *Charlotte* like a magazine, he ran downstairs and

out the front door. (He didn't know where Florence was hiding, but made the assumption she couldn't be too far away.)

Florence had been watching the old wing's door carefully from her spot in the bushes. When the door opened (but no one came out) she immediately guessed it was *invisible Vlad*.

"Vlad?" she called out. "Is that you?"

"Yeah, and I've got Charlotte," he replied.

"I'm down here," Florence then said, standing up enough to allow Vlad to see her.

Vlad quickly went over. He placed Charlotte on the ground (so she could revert to her usual form) and then he turned off his invisibility.

"Is Viv still in the mind reading experimentation room?" Vlad asked.

"I just sent her a message telling her it's safe to move through the tunnel to the old wing," Florence answered. "Mr. Lexington and the scientists won't be leaving that classroom anytime soon, so no one will see her when she exits the tunnel, moves through the first-floor hallways, and comes outside."

...

A few minutes later, Vivian—looking winded—exited the old wing. Vlad stood up and waved her over. (The four detectives were extremely relieved to be reunited, but unsure of what to do from here...)

"Now what?" Vivian asked. "We have no clue how long before Rudd Major will return to pick us up."

"Guess we've gotta find a suitable place to hide," Vlad suggested. "Any suggestions?"

...

"Shh," Florence then said to her team. "I think I hear footsteps."

It was too risky for any of them to pop their heads out from the bushes to see what was going on. (Vlad could try if he went invisible again—but if he were to bump the bushes while moving, it'd make noise and draw unwanted attention.)

...

The steps were getting louder. Someone was walking toward the old wing's entrance (and would presumably open the door to head inside soon.)

All four detectives stayed completely still. (As long as none of them suddenly sneezed or coughed, they'd be fine.)

The footsteps then stopped... (but the door didn't open!)

"I know a place you can hide out," a voice said to the detectives.

The owner of that voice walked around the bushes... it was Mr. Gatwick!

"How did you know—" Florence went to ask.

"All in due time," he replied while squatting down. "I've been keeping an eye on you. ... We've gotta get you somewhere safe to hide until Rudd Major gets back... and I know just the place."

CHAPTER 38

Rudd Major still had his ship traveling at full speed—heading directly for Asos. They knew what the specific goal of their mission was, but ironing out the details of *how to accomplish it* was proving to be very challenging.

In a nutshell, they needed to *"somehow"* destroy the rescue ferry's propulsion system, without getting caught in the process. (If they could severely damage the rescue ferry's engines to a point beyond repair, then the group of imposters aboard it wouldn't be able to continue killing and kidnapping wholphins.)

Zora had come up with a clever way to get on board the ferry again, which was going to require the assistance of President Artez. (President Artez was back at Wholphin Monitoring Headquarters now, so Rudd Major would swing by there to pick her up.)

...

During the flight, Screed spent quite a bit of time teaching Zora a mind reading trick (that Mrs. Beverly had jotted down in the special notebook she secretly gave him in Year 2.) Screed didn't show Zora the book or tell her where he had learned the technique, he just explained the steps he had memorized from those notes.

...

"We'll be landing to get President Artez shortly," Rudd Major announced. "She has already contacted the rescue ferry captain and explained to him the reason we're coming."

"Did the captain buy it?" Dax asked.

"I assume so," Rudd Major replied. "But even if he had his suspicions, he couldn't refuse, as the request had come directly from Asos' leader."

"Ah," Dax nodded. "Saying *'No'* to the president would raise too many red flags, which is the last thing that group of crooks want."

...

Now hovering above the ferry, Rudd Major prepared to start lowering down five people via cables: President Artez, Dr. Loft (who would once again pretend to be the teacher—Mr. Bastilia), Screed, Zora, and Dax.

The captain, his second-in-command, and two other crew were waiting to welcome them and assist in unstrapping the cables.

...

After a round of handshakes, the captain began leading everyone to the large kitchen and eating area—where the entire crew was waiting after having set up the room as instructed. (As far as the crew knew, President Artez, *Mr. Bastilia,* and three of the pupils were here to present an *Outstanding Service Award* from the Asos government for rescuing the students and their teacher who had been adrift at sea.)

Five chairs had been put at the front, all facing the *audience.*

The five "guests" then came in (to a round of applause) and took their seats.

President Artez quickly announced that Screed and *Mr. Bastilia* would be giving short thank you speeches first, and finally the ceremony would finish up with the president presenting a plaque.

Screed was set to go first. He stood up, cleared his throat, and began addressing the crew.

"As some of you may have heard," he began, "I have a medical condition which requires medication to help me manage. When our raft ran out of gas in the middle of nowhere, and I realized I didn't have my medication with me, I started imaging the awful outcomes that might be awaiting… That's when this crew, led by its distinguished captain, miraculously spotted us."

Dax prepared to start "acting" like he was feeling seasick. As Screed continued his speech, Dax—who had intentionally worn extra layers to make him hot enough to sweat profusely—began wiping the sweat from his brow and wiggling around uncomfortably in his seat.

Dax then covered his mouth: making it look like he might be on the verge of vomiting.

Most of the audience had noticed this, so they weren't surprised when Dax stood up and made his way toward the door. (One of the crew who was near the door even opened it so Dax could make it out faster—and presumably run to a toilet or the side railing of the ship—before puking his guts out.)

…

Now out of the kitchen, Dax was free to move around the ship.

Dax knew the shortest route to the engine room. As he quickly moved through hallways and stairs to get below, he sent a short message to Rudd Major.

Heading to the engine room. Wait for my signal.

CHAPTER 39

The scheme they were about to put into action was going to require Rudd Major, Dax, Screed, and Zora to perfectly execute tasks at precise timing.

Having Rudd Major play a part in this was a suggestion made by Captain Mazden—who kept referring to Rudd Major as the *best trick and stunt pilot in the entire galaxy.*

(Shortly after lowering Screed and the other four to the ferry, Rudd Major had ascended to a higher altitude. This wasn't considered strange because it was common practice for hovering ships to not remain too close to ferries or other boats for extended periods of time: as a safety precaution.)

"I still can't believe I let you talk me into doing this," Rudd Major said to Captain Mazden while they waited for Dax's message to arrive. "You know I haven't performed a maneuver like this in decades."

"Doing a trick in an airborne vessel is just like riding a bike," Captain Mazden said, smiling. "Once you learn how to do it, it becomes second nature."

Since the trick Rudd Major was about to perform needed to be done *"without being seen,"* he had turned on his ship's cloak again. (And he was above the clouds when he did that, so there was no way anyone on the ferry would have noticed.)

...

Dax's message then arrived.

> *In the engine room now.*
> *Commence immediately.*

"Your seatbelt on tight?" Rudd Major asked Captain Mazden. "This is gonna be a bumpy ride."

"Ready when you are," Captain Mazden grinned (although appearing a bit nervous now...)

Rudd Major flew his cloaked vessel a few hundred meters away from the ferry, then tilted the nose downward and began reducing altitude.

As he got closer and closer to the ocean's surface, he cranked up his speed.

"You know as well as I do that intergalactic vessels weren't designed to fly underwater," Rudd Major commented.

"But let's not forget," Captain Mazden smiled. "That it was *you* who proved they could."

Using the flight angle he knew would create the smallest splash, Rudd Major flew into the ocean. ... Once he was about 10 or 12 meters deep, he leveled out and aimed toward the ferry.

"I need to slow us down a fair bit," he told Captain Mazden. "To allow us to get a bigger *kick* at the right time."

...

"Almost there," Rudd Major said twenty seconds later. "Get ready for a jolt."

The instant his vessel was almost under the ferry, Rudd Major aimed his vessel perfectly downward to the ocean floor—meaning his two strong engines were now facing directly up, to the bottom of the big ferry.

"Rock and roll," Rudd Major said (repeating a phrase he'd

heard teens use countless times at The Academy.)

Rudd Major pushed the accelerator all the way, rocketing his vessel deeper and deeper into the ocean.

(This rapid acceleration, of course, sent an extremely powerful upward blast right into the ferry's hull.)

* * *

President Artez was halfway through her speech when everyone on board the ferry felt a massive upward jolt (which felt like the ferry had smashed into something big, such as an iceberg.)

Screed and Zora nodded to each other: it was now time to carry out the crucial task they had practiced earlier. (The two detectives were about to perform identical mind-altering tasks—each focusing on a different person. Screed was in charge of infiltrating the captain's mind, and Zora would do the same to the second-in-command.)

(During the speeches, they had both kept close tabs on the location of their respective targets, so they wouldn't have to search for them when this moment arrived.)

Since Screed and Zora had practiced this technique on each other during the flight here, both were confident they could do it effectively right now.

Concentrating on their respective *targets,* Screed and Zora began using a variation of the technique that could mess with people's middle and inner ears: They made the captain and second-in-command think they had heard a loud "metal-scaping-against-something" noise—like that of the hull scraping against an iceberg or a giant rock outcropping.

"Captain!" the second-in-command shouted. "We've crashed into something!"

"That scrape was enormous," the captain said back. "I hope

our hull wasn't cracked in the process."

* * *

Down in the engine room, Dax had waited, as planned, for the instant he felt the jolt.

This ferry's engines powered a single, massive propeller—and that propeller was currently spinning at a relatively slow speed (keeping the ferry moving forward at a velocity of about 4 knots.)

Dax had had his "strong" hand just above the long shaft that attached the engine to the propeller.

"Here goes nothin'," he said softly to himself, gripping the shaft as best as he could.

He clenched his fingers hard on the metal shaft. ... He managed to slow down—and then finally stop—the shaft's rotation. (But the cogs that had been making the shaft move were still trying to do so, meaning excessive pressure was building up in the engine...)

A couple of seconds later, the engine made a loud snapping or cracking noise. Dax let go of the shaft, and smiled when it didn't start spinning again. (The ferry's engines were officially out of commission!)

He then started racing back up to the kitchen, hoping he could get close to it before running into any crew members.

* * *

"Sir!" the second-in-command said to the captain. "We need to get back to the helm. We have probably run into an ice field and we need to navigate through it to prevent any further damage."

"Agreed," the captain replied immediately, looking at the key members of his crew. "Navigator, pilot, follow us to the helm."

But the rest of the crew—including the pilot and navigator—looked confused.

"Didn't you hear the loud snapping noise from deep in the ship?" one of the crew asked the captain.

"I heard our metal hull scraping against something," the captain said back. "But I certainly didn't hear a snap." He then turned to his second-in-command for confirmation.

The second-in-command shrugged his shoulders. "I only heard scraping," he said.

Screed looked over at Zora... They didn't smile (although they both really wanted to!) They were relieved to hear that the noise they'd planted into the ears of the top two people in charge of this ship had successfully prevented those two from noticing the loud *snap* of the engine busting (that everyone else had heard clearly.)

Dr. Loft then began to act panicked—which he did to buy Dax a little more time.

"Before you all start running to your stations," he said, "you need to make sure my pupil is okay. He's probably on a nearby deck, or maybe in a washroom. Someone, please go find him."

The captain—who was about to exit with his second-in-command, pilot, and navigator—nodded to two crew close to the door. (They understood that meant they were tasked with locating the boy.)

* * *

Dax had made it back to the same level as the kitchen, and he was about 20 meters away from its door. The instant he saw the door open, he leaned over the ship's railing, stuck his finger down his throat, and forced himself to cough and then throw up.

"He's right over there!" one of the crew yelled right after exiting the kitchen.

The two crew members helped Dax back to the kitchen. ... Once there, President Artez told the crew that he, the teacher, and the three students would go to the ship's top to get picked up.

(By this time, Rudd Major had flown his vessel back up out of the water to a location above the clouds, and had also turned his cloak off. Nothing would appear odd when he descended to hover above the ferry! They'd done it!)

CHAPTER 40

Back on Vos, Mr. Gatwick had taken Vlad, Charlotte, Vivian, and Florence to the garage-size shed where the school stored the equipment and tools used for tending the large gardens. (The gardening team worked a 1-week-on/1-week-off schedule, so he knew no one would open this shed for the next four days.)

The gardeners had turned the corner of this place into a *mini clubhouse.* There were a few sofas, a coffee table, a small fridge, and a shelf with some board games on it. There were even two fold-out cots that the gardeners used for afternoon naps (particularly on rainy days when they couldn't do any lawn work.)

...

The instant their communicators pinged with a message from Screed—stating that the mission to Asos had been a success and they were on their way back to The Academy—Mr. Gatwick and the four detectives had a small celebration. (The fridge was always stocked with juice, and there were a bunch of cups by the sink.)

"I assume the plan when he gets to Vos," Mr. Gatwick said to the detectives, "is that Rudd Major will cloak his vessel, land close by, and you'll sneak out of here and hop on board?"

"Yup," Vlad answered. "Then he'll fly us back to Zerasta, since our Elite 7 training month is technically still in progress."

"But I doubt we'll be doing any more training," Charlotte commented. "Our top priority will be figuring out what to do about the dirty and dark secrets we uncovered here."

"Well, please feel free to ask me for assistance anytime," Mr. Gatwick smiled. "As you know, I can move around the campus without arousing suspicion."

...

The four detectives seemed as if they had a question (or possibly a series of questions) for the janitor.

"I apologize if this comes off as being too direct," Vlad said. "But what's your... umm, *story?* I mean, you seem to know almost everything. I realize, as the janitor, you probably see a lot... But the way you were able to help us today, and how you also seem to always know where we are and what we're doing, it's just—"

"Excellent inquiry," Mr. Gatwick said, laughing a bit. "You are detectives, and detectives investigate mysteries. ... I can certainly see how my behavior comes across as a bit mysterious."

"We're not accusing you of anything," Vlad quickly added, sensing his comment might have sounded inappropriate. "We're just, well... confused... and curious."

"As you should be," Mr. Gatwick nodded. "Well, I suppose we were going to end up having this conversation at some point, so we might as well do it now. ... To begin with, you'll need to understand something which I have only revealed to Screed. I'll tell you now, but it can't go beyond this room. Well, Zora and Dax can be told, and Rudd Major too, but no one else."

The four detectives nodded in agreement, eager to hear what this announcement was.

"The reason I know so much about your whereabouts and actions," Mr. Gatwick said, "is that I'm a mind reader."

"A mind reader!?" Charlotte reacted. "So, you were a student here, like, 50 or 60 years ago?"

The janitor laughed a bit. "I guess I do look my age," he remarked. "But the answer to your question is *no:* I never stepped foot in here when I was young."

"But every 12-year-old kid who gets a power comes here," Vlad said. "Did you hide your power or something?"

"Yes, I did," Mr. Gatwick admitted.

"Why??" Vlad asked, shocked. "You've got the best power there is! You would've become a Rank 1, and been in charge of missions all over the galaxy. You—"

Vlad stopped talking because he could see Mr. Gatwick was becoming emotional.

"My older brother was born seven-and-a-half years before me," Mr. Gatwick told the detectives. "Are you all familiar with the terms *autistic* and *non-verbal?*"

"Actually," Florence commented. "There was a non-verbal, autistic girl in my class when I was eleven."

"People with autism," Mr. Gatwick went on, "often struggle to thrive because the way they perceive the world, and the way they communicate, is so different from you or me."

"The girl in my class was brilliant," Florence said. "But she was always in her own little world. ... And since she didn't speak, our efforts to communicate with her usually went, umm..."

"You have just described my brother's situation," Mr. Gatwick went on. "We never knew what he wanted, or what he was hoping for, or anything he was thinking, in fact. But that all changed the day I turned 12. When I realized I had mind reading powers, I tried reading his mind... and it worked. I could easily figure out what he wanted.

"And then I made a decision: a decision that I don't regret. I decided to keep my power secret—from everyone, my parents included—and devoted my life to helping my brother. I even learned how to communicate my thoughts to him—a technique very few mind readers have ever mastered."

"Why did you decide to become a janitor at The Academy?" Florence asked.

"My brother passed away six years ago," he answered. "I had no clue what to do with my life. ... I began wondering about the life I had passed up by choosing to hide my power. So, when I saw a job posting here, I figured it'd be a way to, at least to some extent, experience what I missed out on."

"You have a heart of gold, Mr. Gatwick," Charlotte said, walking over and hugging him. "You put the well-being of your brother above your own. Very few people would make that kind of sacrifice."

"Thank you," the teary janitor replied.

"We should rename ourselves the Elite 8," Vlad said, teaching Mr. Gatwick how to do a high-five. "With you as part of our team, we'll crack any mystery."

Vlad then removed his communicator and handed it to the janitor.

"I'll tell Rudd Major to get me a new one," he said to Mr. Gatwick. "We'll send you regular updates, and you can also keep us posted on everything you notice."

"Understood," the janitor grinned, a few tears now sliding down his wrinkly face.

CHAPTER 41

After picking up Vlad and the other three detectives on Vos, Rudd Major flew the entire Elite 7 team, plus President Artez and Captain Mazden, to Zerasta.

Immediately after landing, their two instructors ran outside to welcome back the seven detectives from what had turned from a *"fairly straight-forward mission"* into something much more sinister.

"In our many years as the Elite 7 trainers," Mr. Derringer said to the detectives. "I have never been more impressed or proud."

"Ditto," Ms. Morg added. "You have proven how true the phrase *'age is just a number'* is; You possess the abilities of detectives who have been on active duty for a decade or more."

...

After allowing everyone a chance to shower, they then set up a meeting and *debriefing session* in one of the classrooms with the goal of settling on a concrete plan about what to do from here.

"Thanks to our little trick back on Asos," President Artez said to everyone, "their ability to find and catch new wholphins has thankfully been stopped."

"But only for the time being," Captain Mazden added. "We must assume they won't just *give up:* At some point down the road, they'll get themselves a new ship, and will try to pick up where they left off."

"But let's not forget," Rudd Major said next. "That the beautiful *switcheroo* Charlotte successfully pulled off with the vials has thrown a big wrench into their research."

"There is one thing we haven't done yet, though," Screed mentioned. "We still need to rescue the wholphins from the tank on Vos and return them to their home."

"I hope that will be possible at some point," Vlad said after hearing Screed's comment. "But we certainly can't do it now."

"I agree," Florence said next. "Doing so would be like taking a step backward."

"What do you mean?" Mr. Derringer asked.

"Everything we've accomplished so far," Florence replied, "we did under the radar. They have no clue that we know what's going on. And although I feel guilty about the wholphins being cruelly held in captivity on Vos, trying to save them would be like announcing we have discovered Ms. Flaxton's evil ring of crime."

"But what's wrong with exposing her?" Ms. Morg asked. "She needs to be arrested and removed from her position."

"If we try to have Ms. Flaxton arrested or fired," Screed commented, "it'd backfire on us. Think about it: the *head* of The Interstellar Detective Agency being accused by a bunch of teenagers?"

"She has the authority to permanently expel us from The Academy," Vlad (who knew the ins and outs of procedure and protocol perfectly) added. "And I bet she has enough people secretly working with her that they could make all the evidence vanish without a trace."

"I realize it's not my place to advise," Rudd Major unexpectedly said. "But it seems there is only one option… which is to *do nothing for the time being.*"

"I agree," Screed said right away. "We need to keep our knowledge of this secret. And then we slowly, and carefully, do what we can to learn more."

"I'd say that's the ticket," Vlad said, agreeing with his best friend. "We cautiously gather as much intel as we can, and learn who can be trusted—and when we're finally 100% ready, then we act."

"Hold on," Dax then commented. "So, we just go back to school and act like everything is normal?"

"You got it," Vlad smiled. "And remember, even though we feel like *trained and confident detectives,* we're still only pupils. The curriculum teaches us crucial skills; things we all need to learn. Focusing on our studies is a must: not only for the wholphin situation, but for our lives after graduation as well."

With everyone in agreement that they would *act like they knew nothing* after returning to The Academy, Ms. Morg decided they could adjourn the meeting.

"Now everyone please follow me to the kitchen," she announced. "The instant you told us you'd be coming back, Mr. Derringer and I tried our hand at baking a few cakes. And believe it or not, we succeeded!"

"Woohoo!" Dax cheered, tastebuds ready for some dessert. "I got dibs on the biggest piece!"

…

As they laughed, chatted (and gobbled down cake), Screed took a few steps back to get a clear view of everyone during the mini celebration. He found it fascinating how a group that had so many different skills (and personalities) could mesh into such an effective and capable team.

"Whatcha' thinking about?" Vlad asked Screed after noticing he was deep in thought.

"You remember back when I first found out I had a power?" Screed replied. "And we took a tour of the school? It required a lot of convincing, and a high-tech music room, for me to decide to attend The Academy."

"How could I forget," Vlad answered. "If it wasn't for that music room, I bet I'd be at The Academy on my own."

"Well," Screed said back. "Although my love for music hasn't waned, I can say this... I can, and do, see my future as a detective. The adrenaline from solving mysteries is like nothing else."

"I'll second that," Vlad smiled, high-fiving Screed. "And I'd love to hear more about what changed your mind, but I can see Zora looking your way—and although I can't read minds, it certainly looks to me like she wants some *couple time* with you right now."

"Not only are we Interstellar Detectives," Screed then smiled before walking over to Zora, "but both of us also have girlfriends; Pretty amazing what's happened in the past few years, eh?"

"You got that right, dude," Vlad laughed back, high-fiving Screed again.

Thank you for reading *The Interstellar Detectives 3*. I hope you enjoyed following along as Screed and his friends uncovered a shocking secret while investigating the case of the disappearing wholphins!

And it would be wonderful if you considered adding a review for this book on Amazon or Goodreads. Thank you so much!

If you have any question or comments, please e-mail me anytime (pj@pjnichols.com). I'd love to hear what you think about The Interstellar Detectives' adventures!

Sincerely,

P.J. Nichols

Other Books by P.J. Nichols

P.J. is also the author of two other exciting mystery adventure series. The first series, which is 12 books in total, is about a group of junior high school kids who have to solve baffling puzzles and riddles to save the world from supernatural enemies. The title is:

The Puzzled Mystery Adventure Series

And the second series, which is currently two books but will get longer soon, follows a group of young detectives who take on unbelievably difficult and confusing mysteries on far-off worlds. The title is:

The Unsupers

And... P.J. recently started publishing children's picture books! The titles he has published so far are:

My Outer Space School: My First Week was Cool!

My Outer Space School: Kindness is Cool!

The One and Only Wall Flower: A Tale about Finding Confidence and Being Proud of What Makes You Different

Thank you so much!
PJ

Visit P.J. at www.pjnichols.com

Made in the USA
Monee, IL
11 June 2025